GW00865356

THIS LITTLE WORLD

Stories from Dorset Writers

Edited by Sue Ashby

First published in 2015
By Dorset Writers Network
8 The Orchard
Winfrith Newburgh
Dorset
DT2 8NN

ISBN-13: 978-1518718267
ISBN-10: 1518718264

A CIP catalogue record for this book is available from the British
Library.

CONTENTS

Acknowledgements

This Little World

Acknowledgements

This Little World began as Dorset's Digital Stories and took root in twelve creative writing workshops for adults living in rural areas of the county. We thank the writers who facilitated these events and later read and mentored those adults who submitted their stories: Gail Aldwin, Tracy Baines, Frances Colville, Helen Pizzey, Kate Kelly, Claudia Leaf, Kathy Sharp, Fran Taylor and Pat Yonwin. We were generously hosted by village halls and community venues in Askerswell, Bourton, Cerne Abbas, Crossways, Durweston, Horton, Martinstown, Stalbridge, Sturminster Marshall, Verwood, Upwey and Winfrith Newburgh.

Eight more workshops took place during after-school activities with 11–16 year-old writers. Thanks go to the writers working with this age group: Chantelle Atkins, Tracy Baines, Jennifer Bell, Kate Kelly, Claudia Leaf and Jenny Oliver. And our hosts at Blandford Library, Gillingham School, IPACA, Magna Academy, Portfield Hall, QE Wimborne and Sherborne Girls School. Claysmore School joined in the fun with Year 7 pupils writing their stories as their half-term English project.

The mentoring process was a fascinating one and mentoring writers of all ages has given us the high quality of stories included in this anthology.

Special thanks go to Kathy Sharp who found our title in a book on Thomas Hardy's works written by the literary critic Geoffrey Harvey. "The woodlands represent the Darwinian struggle for existence that Hardy sees as extending not only to the inhabitants of this little world but also beyond." This discovery helped the graphic designers – Tony Benge & Nick Gresham – to create our striking cover. Also thanks to James Manlow and Laura E. James for allowing us to use their photographs on the front cover.

Our thanks go to Helen Baggott, our proofreader who held our hands as we launched into the unknown territory of publication.

We'd like to thank Dorset Libraries for partnering us in launching the community workshops that kick-started this – our first publication – and worked with us to celebrate the launch of the book itself.

This project wouldn't have been possible without all those

creative people out there young and old who love writing, either alone or as a member of the many creative groups around the county, and responded to the challenge of a 500 word story set in Dorset.

Finally, we have to thank the generous individual donors, Dorset Community Foundation and The Arts Council Lottery Fund for giving us, and the writing community of Dorset, the opportunity to create *This Little World*.

Sue Ashby

The photographic images on the front and back covers are acknowledged below:

https://commons.wikimedia.org/wiki/File:Lulworth_-_Durdle_Door_at_English_Channel.jpg

https://www.flickr.com/photos/cathedraljack/15954163327

https://www.flickr.com/photos/danrocha/20306547582

https://www.flickr.com/photos/danrocha/16588533359

https://www.flickr.com/photos/hirezimages/3232250360/

https://www.flickr.com/photos/mvannorden/8275084353

https://www.flickr.com/photos/mvannorden/8276149954

https://ianbeckblog.wordpress.com/2012/03/21/janet-stone-photographs/sylvia-townsend-warner-with-cat-2/

https://www.flickr.com/photos/49580580@N02/6148917782/

NORTH

Ringing the Changes
by
Anne Tillin

The goose grey mist curled through skeletal fingers of trees which scratched against a leaden sky, beneath her feet the grass was winter dry, crisp with a dusting of frost. Alice paused when she reached the top of the hill and as she always did, slowly revolved to take in the magnificence of the landscape spread out before her. Wreathed in coils of chiffon mist stood her favourite landmark Win Green, her eyes followed the curve of hills and bare fields dropping away from its skirts until they rested on the hedges and jumps at her feet.

And the memories flooded her again, the sound of hooves pounding on the track, her two young daughters standing on the bonnet of the car, faces alight with excitement and beside her, his warm hand encompassing hers, the man she had shared her life with for so many years. It all seemed so long ago and as the chill from the ground crept into her boots she dashed a tear away and started to walk into the silent wood.

Twilight gloom stalked the trees, the pond lay still, its steely surface broken by the occasional ripple. Alice perched on a mossy log and recalled long ago picnics, the old plaid blanket, Marmite sandwiches and jam tarts, their children playing hide and seek whilst she and Justin leaned contentedly into one another.

Alice swallowed the hard lump in her throat and was about to continue on her walk when the sharp crack of a twig rooted her to the spot. Shapes shifted in the swirling mist as she peered anxiously towards the sound. Was that a movement, a figure? Heart pounding, Alice began to back slowly away from the looming shadow, her mouth too dry to call out, the silence a thick blanket pressing down. Just then a ray of sunlight pierced the glade and Alice realised that the intruder regarding her with deep brown eyes was as nervous as she was; a soft snuffling came from his nostrils as he tried to pick up her scent. For what seemed an age they stood looking at each other until with a snort the deer turned and bounded away.

Alice walked on through the wood, her fear turned to elation at the encounter, her reminiscences fading as she stepped out into the sunshine and gazed across the valley towards the distant coastline and the hills of Purbeck. A figure appeared at the bottom of the ring accompanied by two black dogs and Alice brought her focus to the man walking towards her, the familiar gait and thick dark hair now dusted with grey, he raised an arm in greeting and she waved back. She watched Justin clamber over the stile, rather less elegantly than in the past, Alice reflected with a smile as she hurried to join him.

A skylark rose singing its way into the sky as they walked towards the beech avenue and, floating through the mist, distant church bells rang the changes.

The Poet
by
Ingrid Hayes

I usually journeyed to the Winterbourne Valley at the height of summer but this year my inclination was to leave it a little later as in recent years my bones felt every stoned step. My stick, used previously as a weapon for stray branches had now become my crutch observed in so many old people determined to battle through paths that had once been sturdily trod in youth. On this particular morning a little autumnal breeze stirred and rippled along the hedgerow and late September's uncertainty made me hesitant about my planned arrival at Stickland where my daughter awaited.

I reached the familiar turn in the lane and halted momentarily, satisfied that I had made good time; this achievement, indeed, propelled my old bones along the final part of the journey. I soon approached the deserted hamlet of Milton where in my distant youth I had spent many an hour under false pretences trying to catch a glimpse of the fair school mistress. It is strange how age allows us to frame most vividly a moment in time, tempting us to still believe in the potency of youth. Beyond the old school house set high from the road a large house stood, below which was a steep embankment crossed with entwined tree roots from where I could hear children shout. The house framed by ripened orchards beckoned me on; I had to open the door and step upon the slated earth, step into the drawing room where I had waited so many years before for her answer… The empty rooms felt tomblike and the only sound was the shrill croaking of half-grown rooklings.

I had not noticed the grey figure in a high-backed chair bent over what seemed to be a printed tapestry. She raised her glassed eyes, smiled benignly then turned to the window.

"Aye it's a thing of beauty – the orchard yonder – at this time of year when leaves crisp upon the bough. Do you remember the young maid cut down before she herself could bear the fruit of youthful passion? How she was sent to float upon the Stour's greened waters in the hope her family could drown their shame in tragic accident. Well, Mr Poet, when you meditate upon the dancing light of the swirling currents and the kingfisher who hovers along the muddy banks, think upon that fair maid whose watery grave can never have an inscription so fine as you would write. What lies beneath those waters of the past is loss and heartache which even your readers can lightly touch with gloved minds."

I leant upon my stick unsure of how to answer, the past staining my present; words I had written with a natural voice now seemed artifice to my dimming light.

I resumed my way to Stickland, my strides now heavy with shortened breath. Where once I had trod with youthful heart and innocent enjoyment I could now only sense the quiet rooks in their listening blackness.

Uplifted
by
Carol Waterkeyn

Annie opened the birthday card from her son. 'Happy birthday and be ready at 5.30am tomorrow for your surprise. Wear warm clothes and sensible shoes, love Jamie x'.

How intriguing. The request for warm clothes and sensible shoes sounded like they were going for a walk in the Dorset countryside. She supposed, with a sigh, now that she was fifty she should get used to sensible shoes.

***

"Morning, Mum. Are you ready?" said a beaming James ushering her to his car.

"Yes, but you are making me a little worried. Where are we going?"

"Let's just say we are going somewhere where the view is magnificent." He smiled broadly.

Annie tried to work out where they were heading. They eventually stopped in Shaftesbury where a Land Rover was waiting. Annie read the sign written on the side of the vehicle and gulped.

"Jamie, I don't think I can do this."

On arrival at their destination, a bright red hot-air balloon was already being inflated. The group they joined went through a safety drill and then they all climbed into the basket. Her son persuaded her that all would be well and she didn't want to disappoint him. She really should get a grip. The six others looked even more nervous than she did.

A loud roar made Annie gasp as the pilot released the propane into the balloon and they started to move. The tethered basket released and immediately they were soaring up, up, up. Steeling herself, Annie opened her eyes as she'd had them scrunched up tight. She grabbed James's arm as the wind blew through her hair and her knees shook. Terrified, she stole a look down and breathed deeply. Annie could see sheep – like white polka dots on the green fabric of fields.

"Look over there, Mum," said Jamie, pointing. A skein of geese were threading their way through the clouds and honking loudly.

They drifted over Cranborne Chase. She could see the earth mounds that the ancient people had built to bury their dead, then a river, and then the sea at Christchurch glistening in the distance with the outline of land beyond. It was as if time had stopped still; it was so peaceful a thousand feet up away from the everyday stresses of life. She felt more alive than she had for a long time and spoke animatedly.

"Oh Jamie, this is the best birthday present ever; how clever of you."

Far too quickly, the pilot said they would be starting their descent. By now, everyone was smiling, and the green undulating ground approached swiftly. They touched down, the basket creaked and the balloon softened around them.

The passengers all climbed out and walked to a small gazebo where champagne was set up for them. James clinked Annie's glass. "Happy birthday, Mum, and many happy returns."

Annie looked pensive for a moment, and then laughed. "Talking of returns, when can we do this again?"

The Roman Hill
by
Alfred

It was another dry and sunny day in north Dorset. Luke decided to walk up Hambledon Hill and try to fly his kite. It was a light purple Flexifoil Stacker Six, one of the best kites available. Luke had decided to go up the doctor's surgery route because he liked walking through a small forest path at the beginning of the hill. When he got to the gate at the top of the path he started to climb up the steepest route, using the old steps cut into the hillside.

He got to the first rampart and walked towards the old fort. The wind was picking up as he climbed higher. He planned to fly his kite from one of the old burial mounds. It took him a little while to get there because it was quite steep. He took his kite out of his new rucksack, and as he bent to unwind the string he saw an old coin a few metres away.

***

Lucius lived in the Roman fort on Hod Hill but had run away from the fighting to be free with the birds. He wanted to live in the ancient remains on Hambledon, left over from an earlier time. He had dug out the steps which he used every time he went there.

Lucius lay on his back gazing up at the clouds. He thought about what had happened last night. The attack on their home had shocked him. He knew they were hated but had not realised it would come to this. He had smelt the smoke first and had nearly choked. He could hear the cattle stampeding in panic and the cows calling to their calves. His parents had escaped but they had had to fight their way out. Luckily for Lucius he remembered the path through the woods, the log over the river and the route up to

9

Hambledon.

He was not sure what to do next. He thought they might come to get him but he did not want to leave the area where he had grown up. His parents were Roman citizens but he felt he belonged here in the ancient fort. He looked through his belongings: a knife, some stale bread and a purse with a few silver coins, including a denarius he had found on the hill some months back. He had always wondered who had dropped it.

***

Luke turned the coin in his hand. He had a strange feeling he recognised it; maybe it was the slight smudge on one side or the small chip on the other. The hill looked lovely in the sunshine as he turned to get his kite ready. The ramparts and the old gate house suggested it had once been a violent, savage place but it seemed so peaceful now. Somewhere in the distance he could still hear a cow calling its calf.

The Price of Beauty
by
Marianne Ashurst

My journey from London to Milton Abbey, being made longer by my horse going lame, lent me time to reflect on my old friend's life. Had Joseph been right to act as he did?

I was hurried to the Earl's bedroom as his trusted physician, and saw at once that I had come to Joseph Damer's deathbed.

"Thomas," he croaked, turning sunken eyes towards me. "Am I… done for?"

The First Earl of Dorchester was not a man to be deceived.

I nodded. "You are being called to your rest, my lord."

The bones stood out through thin, grey skin on the hand he slowly raised from the bed to wave away those gathered. Each breath pained him now, the voice weak and laboured.

"Thomas… my… confession? No time… for priest."

"Whatever you require of me, my lord," I replied. If I could not help his tortured body, perhaps I could ease his mind.

"I've been a man of…" I leaned closer to catch his words. "Vision. Beauty… too much… ugliness in this world."

A tear slid down his bloodless cheek. I imagined his thoughts must dwell on the early death of his beloved Caroline and the tragic loss of his son and heir.

"Your village will be renowned for many generations to come," I agreed, and truly meant it. The people may be as poor as ever but they lived in a village where order and harmony reigned.

"Ah, Milton Abbas," he sighed. "But the park… the church… my legacy." He paused, then forced himself on: "William Harrison… on my conscience. Did him wrong."

I understood immediately what he meant.

"Ah, the lawyer. He was as stubborn as you." I shook my head, thinking back to Joseph's dream for the Milton estate, that he would create a parkland to be envied. I also remembered the old village, a higgle-piggle of untidy dwellings, an eyesore sitting squarely in the middle of his land.

"You were true to your vision," I continued gently. Indeed, I had admired the boldness of his scheme in rebuilding the village at a new site, well out of view. By one means or another most villagers were persuaded to move. Not so William Harrison. He stood by his rights and stayed on his family's land.

The dying earl stirred and plucked at my sleeve. "He refused... me. No choice... had... to... act."

"You had your reasons." I nodded, remembering how, enraged by William's opposition, the earl took drastic action. He ordered the sluice gates of the Abbey pond be opened and flooded the lawyer out.

"I'm sorry... William... I'm sorry," the dying Joseph whispered.

Next morning I visited the Abbey church, knelt by Joseph's elegant monument to Caroline, and prayed for the soul so lately fled.

That his work will stand the test of time, I was certain. Visitors may wonder about the man who let nothing stand in his way. I hoped he fared well, as he stands now before the only one who can judge him.

One Day in Spring
by
Alison Scott

She had been born in the Tarrant Valley near Blandford and had never strayed very far. It was home. Now she was expecting her first baby and could feel it stirring within her. She was content. This was her life, so like that of generations before.

It was early morning and the birds were singing. The winter was really over and new growth on the plants and trees and the abundance of spring flowers gave her pleasure. She wandered out of the garden and across the track into the woods. There was no hurry, nothing else that had to be done. After a while she was aware that she was in an area she hadn't been in for a few weeks. It was quiet and calm, barely a breeze. A bramble brushed against her leg, an irritation. No. Not a bramble, her leg was caught. She jerked her leg to free it but it cut into her leg, becoming increasingly tight.

She pulled and jumped, twisted and bent, to no avail. Her mother and sister would come looking for her. She listened out for them. She tried again and again to free herself but it just got tighter and tighter. The pain shooting through her body was unbearable, her fear increasing, the new life in her belly sensing her distress. The more she tried to free herself, the worse her situation became.

The sun was high in the sky by now, above the canopy, its rays dappling the foliage. But it was of no comfort. She lay still for a while, her breathing laboured and her heart racing, before desperately trying once more to free herself.

The night was long as she drifted in and out of consciousness and no help came. Owls called to each other as if all was well, but it was far from well. As dawn broke on another beautiful day, she had all but given up. The pain was excruciating – her fear, worse.

A sound – a movement – and he was there, looking at her dispassionately with cold blue eyes. With the last of her strength she made a final, frantic effort to break loose, pain lessened by her absolute terror and desperate need to escape. But there was no escape.

A few days later, a young couple, she nearing the end of her first pregnancy, went to a pub in the valley for lunch. As they were perusing the menu, the owner came to their table. With a smile that did not quite reach his cold blue eyes, he recommended the venison, which he assured them was fresh and local.

They declined. There was something about it that did not feel right.

On Bulbarrow Hill
by
Richard Hewitt

"I love it here," he tells her. "It's such a magnificent view."

And it is a magnificent view. The Blackmore Vale spread out immediately below, and beyond to the Somerset Levels, Glastonbury Tor, and in the far distance, on a really clear day, a smudge of what might be the Welsh coastline beyond the Severn.

"Well, it's a magnificent view during the daytime of course," he continues. He knows she will not answer. She hasn't been able to use words for over two years, but he can happily sit in silence with her as he has done many times, enjoying the vista together.

They have often visited the place during their life in Dorset. In the summer the spot is shaded from the sun by trees, which, as the seasons turn, serve as shelter from the south-westerly winds. In all but the greyest of days the view is astounding.

At night the place takes on a different mantle, but no less magnificent. The stars wheel through the heavens in majestic cycles, unspoilt by artificial light, a humbling perspective on humanity's universal position.

No other place can compare with this spot, so it is here the couple come whenever life is difficult, or they have problems to solve. Over the years they have walked the area extensively, but for the last few years, only come to sit and take in the view. Perhaps they eat a picnic lunch, drink from a Thermos, or just sit and gaze.

Lately, they have been coming much more frequently. It is the one place he is sure she will enjoy visiting, and where he can find some solace.

He gets out of the car. "The sky is marvellous, I'm sure that's Jupiter in the west," he observes as he begins his

15

night's labour.

"Well, I've sure worked up a sweat now," he says, panting a little, as he opens the passenger door. He slips his arms under her knees and around her shoulders and lifts her from the car. She doesn't resist. Her head falls against his shoulder as he straightens, just as it did forty-two years ago when he had carried her over the threshold.

Tears smart his eyes as his words catch in his throat. "You always said you could spend eternity here," he sobs as he gently lowers her lifeless body into the newly dug grave.

A Town I will never Forget
by
Louise Bliss

The letter said, *three o'clock.* I approach the bridge, I glance to my left, trees framing the Crown Meadows, the river Stour meandering through. Whatever the season, that scene never fails to disappoint. In the distance The Crown, a welcome sight after a walk through Bryanston Woods.

"Meet me outside The Crown," he'd say. I thought he must be posh. As children we just used to push our noses up against its fancy windows; we never went in.

I do not stop, this is not the meeting place.

I walk up West Street towards Market Place. Wall-to-wall Georgian architecture. I remember Mr Simpkins, our school teacher, telling us how lucky we were to live in a real-life Georgian museum; it was like someone had sprinkled fairy dust to preserve it in an extraordinary period of time.

I continue up Salisbury Street. I can see the men marching proudly, wearing their uniforms. The streets start to quieten and the sun is fading. I am late, but I do not hurry.

A turn right takes me into the Plocks and I admire the beautiful craftsmanship of Lime Trees and Coupar House, both now Listed and proudly displaying their blue plaques. There is something magical about this place. Is it the people, or is it the past that continues to be part of the present?

My feet seem to have a will of their own today. I find myself standing outside the Old House. You could easily hurry past, but once it catches your attention you want to know more: How old is it? Who lived there? How did it survive the great fire of 1731? Before too long I find myself staring up at the cupola of the church and wondering what the Bastard brothers would think of the town today.

So many questions, so many questions. I do not think it

will ever get any easier. I arrive at the meeting place. "I am here, Jack," I whisper. There is no reply and I know there never will be. I am late.

Not just ten minutes or even a few hours, I am seventy-five years too late.

11th May 1940
My Dearest Kitty,
Meet me outside the Corn Exchange tomorrow at three o'clock. I have something very important to ask you.
Love always, Jack x

I never did receive the letter. Why? Why did my father do it? Why tell me when it was too late? Too late for me, and certainly too late for Jack.

Our meeting place, the Blandford Corn Exchange, will be forever etched in my memory. That day should have been the first day of the rest of our lives.

I lay down my poppy wreath and card: *Love always, Miss Kitty Minterne x*

I say a prayer and leave.

A Bit of a Week
by
Rachael Calloway

Ever since her husband had passed away, she had made this same trip every single Thursday. Never had it felt like this.

The same white vans lined the side of the High Street. Familiar market traders bantered with customers. The usual products jostled for space on the stalls, but today she did not stop for her piece of plaice or her three soil-dusted carrots. Instead, she hurried straight down the hill to her favourite café. Her unusually empty shopping trolley bounced behind her, wobbly wheels clattering in noisy protestation. Her trolley was light but her heart sagged heavily.

She pushed through the steamed-up door and was pleased to see an empty table. She arranged her coat on the back of the chair as a sign to others that the place was taken. Today she was not interested in the usual chit-chat with the regulars. She needed time to think; time to un-jumble the tangle of thoughts in her head.

She worked her way along the rows of glass domes, Darwinesque specimens exhibited within. The cake species had evolved rapidly in the past few years. No rock cakes, no Eccles or Battenberg. Even fairy cakes had turned into 'cupcakes'. But she wasn't complaining; there was always something new to tempt her.

She wasn't particularly hungry after the week's events, but routine had forced her here. She was glad. The warm cosiness of the café was like a pair of soothing arms wrapped around her. She reflected on the fact that she had no one to comfort her anymore.

She listened in on a conversation. Two men were discussing the previous week's EuroMillions. "Seventy-two million! What would someone do with all that? It's obscene."

"Build a new hospital," said one man, prodding the table with his finger to make his point.

"Cancer research," said the other. "They could probably cure cancer with that lot."

She sat still, mouth hovering over the froth of her drink and then slowly placed her cup on to its saucer. She reached into her bag and hastily scribbled a note, which she slid under her saucer.

When she went to pay, the waitress glanced at her untouched cake and looked at her quizzically. "You look very pale today. Can I call someone to come and take you home?"

She managed a weak smile and reassured the waitress that everything was fine. "It's been a bit of a week," she said. As she stepped outside, she paused to look in at the men. "Thank you," she whispered and began the climb up Shaftesbury High Street.

She thought about her week: diagnosed with terminal cancer Monday, winning the EuroMillions Tuesday. At least she now knew what to do with the money; cancer research would make good use of it. Smiling to herself she headed home, wondering if the waitress had cleared the table yet. Wondering if she had found the fifty pound tip and the note that said, 'Thank you for caring'.

Sunday 14th February
by
Christine Diment

"'Tis strange he's not 'ere," whispered Old Tom. It was silent in the tiny mediaeval church. They had been waiting for over half an hour. There was a restless shuffling of feet on the cold stone-flagged floor. The vicar was never late. He had never missed a service in thirty years. Snow was falling silently in the small graveyard of St Andrew's Church. Every Sunday, Reverend Tobias Wilmott walked two miles from the neighbouring village of Bloxworth to the tiny hamlet of Winterborne Tomson.

"Come rain, come shine, come wind, come snow, he'll be 'ere," muttered George as he watched a few random snowflakes swirling in the cold northerly wind outside. There was an eerie silence apart from the mournful lowing of the cattle in the stalls adjacent to the flint church and the ominous calls of the crows high up in the nearby beech trees. The tiny congregation consisted of a handful of people living in the few cottages and the farm clustered round the church. They sat in contemplative silence, only the tops of their heads and the few black bonnets showing above the high box pews.

"I think I'll go a look for 'im," whispered Old Tom again.

"I'll come too," added George as he stood up and made his way to the studded wooden door.

Outside, a few snowdrops peeped through the thin layer of snow in the small churchyard. It was 14th February, St Valentine's Day. Old Tom pulled his jacket tighter around him as the cold wind blew across the open fields. The two farm labourers made their way along the track, bent double against the biting wind. After about a mile they stopped suddenly. There in front of them, in the middle of the track, was a black hat and a walking cane. Old Tom bent over to examine them more carefully. He recognised the cane with its silver ball handle. They belonged to Reverend Tobias. Every Sunday, when the Reverend entered the church, he would carefully place his cane and hat just inside the entrance, next to the stone font on the right. George and Old Tom always sat at the back of the church and would observe this ritual from their pew. Tom picked up the hat. A single red rose lay on the snow beneath it.

"'Tis strange," he said quietly. There were no footprints in the snow. There was no sign of any other disturbance.

No-one ever discovered what had happened that day. Reverend Tobias had disappeared. Every year since then, on 14th February, the Reverend's hat and silver-handled cane appear next to the old stone font in the tiny church of St Andrew's. No-one knows who puts them there or who takes them away.

A single red rose lies under his hat.

The Length and Breadth...
by
Mike Chapman

Stourhead is the start. It is where Dad, so wiry and strong
until asbestosis, would walk reciting the Latin names of the
trees and taking the colours back home for his sketchbook
during winter evenings. I walk with the dog now through
the ancient woods and combes to Bourton where the old
foundry lies wrecked. Its ruination evokes Grandpa's awful
stories about Gallipoli where, with faith in the fuses, he
would hold those Mills bombs in his home-made catapult
just long enough to burst over the Turkish trenches.

On south to the bridge at Sturminster Newton where I
would threaten young J with transportation to Australia if
he wasn't terribly good and where we wondered at the scale
and power of floods a quarter of a mile wide. He and I, as a
proper dad for once, would walk the meadows to the weir at
Cutt Mill where no one went, where the kingfishers fished at
will and where the sun baked the lush fields so we could
hardly breathe.

With grudging thanks to Beeching – imagine, the bridges
destroyed so policy could not be changed – I now cycle the
trailway towards Blandford: trout in the river, steam trains
at Shillingstone, Iron Age forts to the left, the heights of
Bulbarrow to the right. There are no finer views than the
Blackmore Vale from Bulbarrow or the 360 degrees from
Hod Hill: Poole to Glastonbury, the hills of Somerset to the
scarp face of Cranborne Chase. Those Iron Age boys knew a
thing or two about location.

More old fort at Badbury where twice a year we would
bet on the horses racing on the downs; a mile to oh-so-
elegant Kingston Lacy where J's granddad had manned the
ack-ack in the war but where now we go just to see the
snowdrops; on to the glory of Wimborne Minster and then

the noise of Hurn, where first I lived when I moved south-west. What full, energetic days they became for me released thus from a dull Midlands nightmare. I felt I had gone abroad again, back to the sunshine.

The river now has well-defined banks, structured walks and even a golf course as it skirts the outer arms of the spiral galaxy that is Bournemouth, then on past the quay with its ever-hungry swans, past the Priory and, at last, into Christchurch Harbour. This by way of the boat-filled channel alongside Stanpit Marsh where I fell in love with my beautiful new girl whilst we watched the birds and the horses, all as wild and remote as the Camargue itself (first seen, of course, as kids during a summer holiday chasing round the Roman legacy in the south of France in Dad's old Austin).

In this same spirit, we bought a canoe together and mounted our own middle-aged expeditions across the harbour to Hengistbury Head with a renewed sense of achievement and discovery in starting over as ever those first Phoenicians landing there.

SOUTH

Horizons
by
Marlene Heinrich

Home was noisy, dirty, unfriendly: Lulworth – cliffs, birds, beaches.

Andrew liked the way the cove was nearly a circle. Standing near the cliff's edge, he'd imagine smugglers from before, or shipwrecks. Sometimes, avoiding prickly gorse, he'd pretend to be a poacher. Once he'd even seen a snake, sunning itself on a stone! Then one day there it was – a green glass bottle, washing backwards and forwards in the sea. Something made him wade in, untangle it from stringy seaweed and take it back to the shore. He flopped down. Not until the pebbles were digging into his skin did he realise an idea had formed. The bottle itself wanted him to join in a game it needed to continue, with a life of its own.

This silent communication – between boy and bottle – was interrupted by a noisy helicopter.

Coastguards, he thought, but didn't look up.

Peace, brought by the gently breaking waves, returned. He scanned the tideline for treasures.

First to go in the bottle was a worn, twisted piece of twig, blackened by fire; then a piece of blue plastic with the remains of an 'A' – his initial – printed on it. A razor shell wouldn't fit but two small pebbles would. He hesitated. What else could help carry on with the game?

A seagull's cry pierced the sky. He looked up. Inspiration! I know, he thought excitedly, moving over to his clothes, flung on the beach. A multi-coloured marble was pulled from a pocket. That'll catch the light of the sun! It ceremoniously joined the other players in his game. Now the stopper. Easy. Plenty of rubbish bits around...

"Andrew!" his mother, calling. He had to hurry. Finishing the stopper and tightly securing it with an elastic band from his other pocket, he replaced the green glass bottle containing 'memories, Lulworth Beach 1998', back into the sea. Watching it eaten up by the waves, he muttered: "We'll meet again. I know it."

That was three summers ago and here he was, hoping for some kind of reunion with his green glass accomplice. He stood, again amazed by the beauty of the cove, and watched a flock of seagulls over a shoal of fish. A boat was being clumsily rowed a short distance away. He heard the softness of the lapping and breaking of the waves.

Then he saw it. The sunlight glinting on something in the water. Smiling, he couldn't suppress his happiness. He ran in, plunging hurriedly towards it, eyes fixed on the bobbing object... but no small glass green bottle. Just a slightly cracked, plastic bottle. No enchantment. No reunion. Only the disillusionment his life was already carrying. Feeling cracked and empty like the plastic bottle, he waded ashore, flopped on the beach and almost started to cry – but not quite.

"We'll meet again. I know it – I just know it!" He remembered, and as if in answer, a wave broke on the shore – incomplete.

October Journey
by
Mary Bevan

The old wooden signpost was half covered with greenery and in need of repainting, but Kurt saw it just in time. *Moreton Village* it said, pointing to a small road off to the left. The year was turning from summer to autumn but still wild flowers were everywhere. Rounding a bend he came upon it, just as the websites promised – the old school house, Lawrence of Arabia's grave to his right, and to his left the white Dorset Gate leading to the church he had come from his home in Germany to visit.

His grandfather never saw it like this, only flew over it in the dark, focused on finding his target – probably the nearby RAF base – and getting out again. He had not found it; instead, if the records were correct, his bomb had fallen on Moreton's little medieval church, destroying the north wall and shattering the stained glass. It was this church, rebuilt, with its extraordinary windows etched by Laurence Whistler, that Kurt had come on pilgrimage to see, seventy-four years to the day that the bomb hit.

Coming in from the sunshine, he expected the church to seem dark. He was wrong. Light exploded from the arched windows all around him. And every window was alive with movement. Etched behind the altar, great candles seemed to flicker as the sun came and went behind them. Around him in other windows sparkled flowers, butterflies, stars, planets, a country house in a snowstorm, a field of harvested corn, the wreckage of an English Spitfire, birds circling in a sky criss-crossed with vapour trails. He stood transfixed.

One picture in particular he must find. And there it was – this church in ruins on the 8th October, 1940. Unexpected tears welled up. Here, hundreds of miles from his home, his grandfather – his Opa who had given his life for the

29

Fatherland somewhere in the skies over England – was written into history in this little church. He sat in a pew and lost himself in contemplation of all that meant. Silence more resonant than speech wrapped around him.

After a while he stirred. He had another thing to do. Making his way round the outside of the church he found the pane of dark glass he was looking for. As he gazed, a shadowy figure came into focus – Judas hanging, thirty pieces of silver dropping from his lifeless hand. An embodiment of pain and suffering, like the pain and suffering of war. But not entirely, for he saw now that Judas' face was turned towards a great light streaming down on him. So this was why Whistler had called it his Forgiveness Window. And as the silver coins touched the earth they were turning to flowers. So also one night long ago his grandfather had destroyed this place, but it had blossomed again in beauty and reconciliation. Mutual forgiveness is all.

He had found so much more here than he had expected. "God bless, Opa," he murmured.

Free Wheeling
by
Laura

Katherine battled with the pedals on her new bike. She had not quite got used to the bike yet with its gears and fancy suspension. It was all new to her. Coming up to a sharp bend in the road she eased the handlebars carefully around the corner. The bike wobbled slightly, no longer travelling in its usual straight line. Katherine looked at her shadow and smiled. She could see herself – four years old and on her first cycling outing. She had only just learnt to ride her bike without stabilisers and Dad was running alongside her. She was still getting used to the balancing part and still wobbled occasionally.

As she turned the corner, the road became an uphill. She inwardly groaned. Her legs were already tired and did not have the strength quite yet to take on such a hill. Exhausted with the effort and panting like a dog, she pulled over to the side of the road. Cars filtered past and a couple of cyclists came rocketing down the hill towards her. She giggled at their excitement and pleasure. She would go up the hill – but just so she could see the castle for a minute and then she would go down it again! With a new burst of energy she set off again to the top of the hill. Reaching the top, Katherine dismounted and looked down on to Corfe Castle. It looked even more magical than ever. The evening glow of the sun outlined it to perfection. Katherine could imagine how powerful the castle must have looked before it had been destroyed. All her childhood memories flooded back, picnics on the hill, exploring the castle, trying out archery and even a little bit of play sword fighting! The memories were still alive, as strong as ever. She recalled the first time she had seen the castle from the hill and the times she had pretended that she was a princess living at the castle. She remembered strolling through the castle grounds, imagining everyone she saw was her servant. To Katherine, Corfe Castle was the most magical place in the world.

At last she turned from the view and mounting her bike once more she started to go down the hill. Faster and faster the bike went, just like the first time she had ridden this road. There were no brakes for her today. She was flying. She turned her face to the last rays of the sun and let its fading warmth flood through her. She might now be nearly seventy and no longer the four-year-old of her shadow but it was no different; it was still as fun as the first time she had cycled up and down the hill and seen the castle.

Goodbye, Goodbye
by
Jane Wade

On a bleak day in Swanage it's the painting that finds me,
not the other way round. A lonely beach under an autumnal
sky, tucked inside a softwood frame; it is as though I've been
brought here just to see it through the shop window. It takes
me back forty years.

We were just kids at the seaside and the day was
mournful, the sky as overcast as heavy metal that might fall
at any moment in sheets of rain. That was what it had felt
like sometimes, on holiday when we were young. Me and
my brother. Hoping for a blue sky swarming with birdsong
so that we could swim, because without it the push and pull
tide would be too cold for our tender white knees. At least
that's what Mum had told us.

We walked along the sand instead, dressed and dry and
skimming stones; watching them jump and bounce and sink;
watching the smouldering sky and hoping. And after a
while the beach curved away and took Mum with it. We had
left her on a deckchair, sitting beneath a straw hat that she
wore as a prayer for the sun, its blue ribbon flying out like
the tail of a kite. She had vanished and the beach was empty
except for us, standing with our backs to the sea. The chill
was all around: it fell from the sky and climbed from the
ground. I started to shiver, but my brother began to run.

He ran until the sound of his feet faded. I put up my
hood and turned away, and I was alone. I could no longer
see him, I could no longer hear him; and for a while I was
afraid. And then exhilarated. I had been bequeathed the
beach, the sea, the grumbling sky by everyone who had ever
walked upon it, swam in it, lain beneath it. Gulls were
crying goodbye, goodbye; they flew to the horizon on
quotation mark wings, and all that remained was the

whippy wind that scurried fine sand up my sleeves.

Mum still sat in the deckchair, the blue ribbon fidgeting in the breeze that we brought back with us. My brother still wanted to swim, but I had known exhilaration and a metal sky scratched by the beaks of retreating gulls, and for me that was all and everything.

Today my past is an autumn painting on an autumn day; a gunmetal sea and an overcast sky, a struggling sunset and mist creeping up from the sand. I see it clutched by shadows at the back of the shop as though in disgrace. I see a child who was not afraid to be left alone on an empty beach. I pay the young woman at the counter and walk out with bubble-wrapped memories under my arm, and a clutch of gulls call goodbye, goodbye, their wings like quotation marks wrapping secret messages as they fly above the waves.

Never Set Foot
by
Lucy

Let me take you back years ago to Durdle Door, the year is 1715. To you they would have looked like two blinding blue lights swerving through the arch. They flew like ever-floating feathers through crashing waves, framed by the sweep of rock. Their songs filled the desolate beach. Occasionally, beams would reflect against their shimmering scales. They were mermaids – sisters, Tempest and Storm.

The two sisters didn't know of the danger that lurked through the stone doorway of Durdle Door upon the pebbled beach, and strangely, nor did they know of the creatures that threatened them: monsters with land tails and hearts of stone. Monsters armed with terrible weapons: spears, harpoons and heart-piercing arrows. You will know these monsters for they are men.

On this day of which I tell, there were six men. They had heard that the legends were true, that there were mermaids at Durdle Door. They set a watch upon the beach with lanterns to keep the darkness at bay. After the long wait, they gave way to liquor and loud-mouthed laughter.

Drawn by the lights of the lanterns, which looked like fallen stars, Tempest and Storm swam closer. Too close. Suddenly, Storm found herself in a tangle of ever-tightening cords. Tempest watched helplessly as her sister was dragged in netting to the pebbly shore.

***

2015
As you will know, mermaids live for many hundreds of years until they are washed upon heavenly beaches.

And so Tempest lived on, but always the memory of her

sister remained with her. Now Tempest knew that her time was close and she was soon to depart for the heavenly beach. She must have her revenge.

She dove at a rapid speed beyond the boundaries of Lulworth Cove. No-one ever dared to venture there.

Instantly, a cold loneliness swept through her body. Tempest was alone in an alcove near the forbidden shore, a place that felt familiar but mysterious. Her tears turned to salt; her soft curls to mangled knots. Her beauty left her, replaced with an almost incontrollable strength.

Tempest crouched behind a large boulder; first she must lure the men out, then strike in bold recklessness and make them pay.

She let out a beautiful siren tune; her bittersweet hymn echoed over the rolling seas, upon a netting ship, reaching a young fisherman. Tempest's song swept him out of his wits. She stroked his smooth cheek and whispered in his enchanted mind, "Your brothers murdered my sister." All was silent but the crashing waves. "I will have my revenge."

Immediately, a swarm of fuming seamen pawed at her, clutching torture instruments. She had been tricked.

Tempest woke in a tank surrounded by strange instruments.

"Tempest?" An oddly familiar voice pierced her heart. "Storm?"

Amongst the creatures with land tails who peered at her stood her sister with a land tail of her own.

"It's time to join the Master Race, Tempest." Her sister's voice was the sharpest harpoon point. Storm was lost. Lost in a final wave of madness.

A Helping Hand on Ballard Down
by
Tod Argent

I will never forget my first descent of Ballard Down in the Purbeck hills. There I was, just getting my breath after Nine Barrow Down, and ready for the last leg before the roadwork back to Sandbanks and the ferry. Ready for my tea too, ravenously hungry as the December sun started to set, covering the hills in black and red. Ballard Down, here we go. My new hybrid bike was like a horse giving me as much speed as I could handle. I was ready to fly.

Pushing off the top was like a ski run, fast and exhilarating, the cold air rushing at me, my beast of a bike handling like a thoroughbred. I was aiming true for Old Harry when my world turned upside down. The bike bucked and in slow motion the handlebars punched into my helmet. Time stopped and a series of freeze-frames took over.

I was floating, spinning noiselessly watching the sky, the ground, the sea.

Silence. Then a voice.

"I'm Barney." Blue eyes looked out from a weather-beaten face. "Can you see me?" He had a kind voice, with a Dorset lilt to it. "Can you move your legs for me? Now the other one. You've had a bit of a shock alright, but you'll live."

Barney had talked me back on to my feet and was now walking me slowly down to Studland, pushing my bike. "You hit a hefty old stick, unlucky there, it's the shadows this time of night."

Barney was dressed for hiking, about sixty and looked strong.

As I gained strength and confidence we talked. He walked the Dorset coast and beyond, had done the whole

South West Coastal Path from Sandbanks to Minehead. He pointed out the things I hadn't really noticed at the top. Swanage to the west, lying in that bay between the hills, where Alfred the Great had seen off the Danes. Poole Bay to the east, with its grand harbour. Bournemouth, miles and miles of golden beaches, and further east, Hengistbury Head and the Isle of Wight, the Needles guarding its approaches.

At Old Harry Rocks, we stopped and took in the last rays lighting up the white limestone citadels.

"I wish you luck, Rosie," he said, clasping my hands. "Now you better get off, your bike's light is useless and it's nearly dark."

Dad would be worried. I reached for my phone, patted my pockets; it was missing. Barney took my address and set off back to Ballard Down to look for it. What a gentleman he was.

Two days later my phone arrived, and a note.

Dear Rosie, how are you, my brave young lady? Here is your phone. Now promise me you will pause a minute before racing headlong down our lovely hills, and when you ride these tracks again drop me a line, care of the YHA. The highway is my home.

I smiled. So I was right, he was a gentleman after all, a gentleman of the road.

A Life
by
Mona Porte

A thought shafts through my subconscious, like a shard of lightning too elusive to grasp.

I stand on the clifftop in the deepening dusk, staring at the aubergine-black tentacle of rock clawing its way out to sea, the arch beneath outlined by the veiled moon. The rise and fall of my chest harmonises with the suck and scrunch of the waves far below.

I can touch his spirit here. I reach out to caress his cheek, but totter slightly as my hand finds only the empty night air and his face dissolves into the yawning void.

My son crept into being in the shadow of a tombstone; a secret I kept from him. Why sully his life with that scrap of sordid truth? Instead I'd spun a gossamer person from yearnings and plausibilities, creating a perfect avatar father figure.

"What was he like?"

"Loving. Couldn't wait to meet you."

"Do I look like him?"

"You have his eyes. Twinkly. Very attractive to girls." I smiled, bolstering his fragile teenage ego with seeds of self-confidence.

"How did you meet?"

"He came to train at the Gunnery School up at the camp. Going to be a Royal Marine, he was. They're the elite."

His eyes glowed with pride and I knew I'd connected with his psyche. As the years unfolded, his obsession grew. I fleshed out the hazy entity I'd created, with photos from the Internet and left-hand-written letters tied into bundles with pink ribbon.

"Tell me again how he died."

"A hero's death. He threw himself on an I.E.D. Saved the

lives of three comrades."

"I'm going to be brave and daring like him."

"Your father's son," I beamed.

"And he died just before I was born?"

I nodded, shirking those deeply sympathetic eyes lest my own betray the lie.

Now as I stand here, stripped of all that matters, my mind drifts back to the snuffed-out reality of that night.

A gaggle of girls in the pub; we drink shots, becoming more provocative, strutting our stuff. A posse of squaddies sidles up to us; they ply us with booze. The one with the twinkly eyes singles me out, suggests a walk. I'm keen. His arm steadies me as I coggle down the road on my fashionable pinnacles, my tighter-than-tight skirt riding up. I giggle; act girly; allow myself to follow his lead through the lychgate of the church. We lean against the weathered wood, hungry tongues exploring moist mouths. He entices me further in; arms entwined we lurch against a bush, ricochet off it, roll down a slope and land on a flat grave. I feel the moss under my thighs and my head is rammed against the tombstone as we make love.

The next night in the pub, his eye glides over my face, flushed with anticipation. A flicker, near-recognition; then nothing. I'm an erased memory.

My earlier elusive thought crystallizes; I fabricated a life; divine retribution dictates I must forfeit one. My son died yesterday, tombstoning off Durdle Door.

Perspectives
by
Patricia Gallagher

Raised eyebrows followed Kate as she slammed the classroom door shut.

Stupid idea, coming to this 'Personal Growth' weekend. All she really needed was a break from the kids, dog, husband. She marched towards the cove, anticipating walking until her mind emptied of irritating clichés.

Lulworth Cove was bustling and Kate hurried towards the track that led off the main path. Moments later she paused and took a deep breath, relishing the magnificent cliff top scenery and the solitude.

"Would you join me?"

Startled, Kate looked in the direction of the voice and saw an elderly couple stretched out on the rough grass. Kate hesitated for a moment too long.

"I'm Joan and this is Ron."

Ron remained reclining, but Joan was patting a space on the tartan blanket next to her. "I've a story to tell you," she continued. Kate's heart sank. She found herself sitting, forcing an encouraging smile, but the woman was staring out to sea. Kate followed her gaze.

The breeze had stilled and an expectant silence fell. The cliff, the waves below, the great rocky outline of Portland in the distance – all seemed to be waiting to hear the woman's story.

Joan began to speak, as much to the landscape as to Kate. "I nearly lost Ron when we had only just met. It was at the end of the war. I was a nurse at Shaftesbury Military Hospital and he was on my ward – in a bad way. He had TB. He'd told me earlier that week that he wanted to marry me: he sounded as though he meant it. Then he took a turn for the worse, but there was a miracle. It was penicillin, you see.

They were trying it out and Ron got lucky. It was the talk of the hospital, his recovery. But now he's gone."

There was a moment of utter stillness, then Kate suddenly turned to look at Joan. Her eyes were bright with tears. Kate looked over at Ron, appalled as the significance of the words sank in. She jumped up.

"We must call an ambulance!" she cried.

"No dear, look at him. He went about an hour ago, quite peaceful. We had a good life, difficult sometimes when the family came along. I don't have any regrets though. They knew I loved them."

Kate couldn't find any words.

"You go now, dear. I'll sit here a little longer. We used to come here when Ron was convalescing. Would you give me half an hour and then phone someone to come and get us?"

Kate knelt. "I'm so sorry," she finally managed to say.

Joan took her hand. "Don't be. No regrets, remember?"

She reached the cove in a daze. Shock had given way to a sense of urgency. It was her home number that she rang first, *They knew I loved them* echoing in her ears. Kate took a deep breath and prepared to do what she so rarely did. Speak from the heart.

No regrets.

The Tyneham Lad
by
Vivienne Edwards

"Tom." The faintest of whispers alerts my lively senses. Is it Grandpa Tom? The haunting voice pulls me on towards the hollow of Tyneham village; the unique settlement, nestling in the lush, green Purbeck hills.

A rush of warm air engulfs me, exposing the once beating heart of this rugged coastal community, where kinship held sway. This was home for Grandpa; seventeen, and apprenticed blacksmith to his father – until that bitter day in 1943, when the land was requisitioned by the War Office.

Never had Tom imagined leaving, never! Subliminally rootless; he'd absorbed the anger of a people betrayed and forsaken. Purbeck became the painful reminder of a severed umbilical; a displaced people, cut to the marrow.

As Tom's final wish to be buried here is fulfilled, who could dispute the irony? Everyone's gone but me; left with the sting of resentment that grips me fast, as I think of Grandpa, fighting in foreign fields for freedom in Europe.

End of story? Not for me... Like an embryo, the image of a homeland lost in the past has become tantalisingly real; until I can wholly identify with my namesake.

Purposely, I stride the mossy pathways of this ghostly, derelict hamlet; until I reach Grandpa Tom's. The meagre hearth is open to the skies, the jagged stone walls supporting nothing but determined buddleia and invasive ivy. Here Tom lived, cheek by jowl with his parents, brother and sisters... I am choked; crying inwardly for his loss, and mine.

"Tom!" An urgent call comes from the small school house. Keenly I go in, scanning the orderly desks, preserved just as they had been on that fateful day. The spirit of forgotten children fills the room with chatter and excitement in this indelible place of learning. Grandpa Tom is among them; his eyes deep and thoughtful.

After some immeasurable time, I revisit the medieval parish church, where the pungent spring flowers contrast the stark greyness inside. Tom is here too; not in a box, but preciously cradled in his mother's arms, as he is christened with the name we both share... Are we done here?

"Follow me." Grandpa is firmly directing my steps, as eagerly I trail through the dappled tree line. A broad carpet of wild garlic commingles with the fragrant bluebells, heightening my senses with the extravagant timelessness of this place. My pace quickens, as each new breath conveys the distinct taste and smell of salty sea spray. Triumphantly, I mount the sand dunes to the spectacle of rumbling waves in Worbarrow Bay.

I stop: I close my eyes and listen... All at once I get it!

This tiny patch of Dorset has a legacy that goes much deeper than the sand and rock under my feet. In nature there's something profoundly connecting me with Grandpa Tom and all before him. It's always been here, and I'm sure he knows it too. Now it's my time to run with the baton. Tom, the lad from Tyneham, lives on, in me.

Dorset Blue Vinney
by
Robin Wrigley

"Excuse me, miss." It was the red-faced man on table twelve with the extremely thin wife.

"Yes, sir? Can I help you?" Laura was dreading this; her second evening in the restaurant of a small family hotel in Swanage. Instinctively she knew this spelt trouble.

"What type of cheese is this?" he asked somewhat rudely, pointing at his cheese platter.

"I believe it is Blue Vinney, sir," she replied hoping to god that it really was.

"But I distinctly asked for Stilton." His irritation stepped up a level while his wife looked embarrassed as other diners were now paying attention to the situation.

"Oh, that's right," Laura countered regaining her confidence. "The chef said that we did not have any Stilton, sir, and that Blue Vinney is very similar but better. It is locally produced here in Dorset."

"Surely if I asked for Stilton it meant I wanted Stilton, wouldn't it? And, if you didn't have any and chose to serve your own make, doesn't it behove you to at least tell me? Wouldn't you agree?" Laura just stood and stared, her face turning pink; she could sense tears forming in her eyes.

He continued glaring at Laura. His wife muttered something unintelligible and was silenced by his outstretched hand. She began to look even more uncomfortable.

"Excuse me." It was the man from the next table, a lone diner. "I take it you are not from these parts?"

"What's it to you?" He turned to face this new intervention that had been addressed by an elderly man in a wheelchair.

"Well nothing really, I just wondered whether anyone

being as inconsiderate as you, had grown up in this town. You see, I am also a visitor and found the staff here, in particular the young lady serving you, so helpful and was curious. That's all." With that he returned to reading the book that he had open next to his plate.

The red-faced man's face became even redder. Laura continued standing on the spot, searching her brain but nothing came to mind. The man's wife now seemed to be looking for somewhere to hide when all of a sudden her husband stood up. Shoving his chair aside he made as if to leave the room. He got three steps from the table when he collapsed to the floor with an almost imperceptible thud.

The next few moments were a blur of people rushing to the man's side and much cries of, "How awful." Laura and the man's wife burst into tears.

Unexpectedly, a man from table six stood up, announced he was a doctor, and kneeling beside the fallen figure loosened his tie and proceeded to apply mouth to mouth resuscitation, without success.

The manager called through the doorway that an ambulance was on its way. Fifteen minutes later two paramedics appeared in the room and said, "What seems to be the problem?"

"Dorset Blue Vinney," came the reply from the gentleman in the wheelchair.

Out of the Mist
by
Louise

It was early morning and we were the first visitors. The mist hadn't yet cleared from Corfe Castle, slithering in and out of the ruins. We could just discern the old drawbridge amidst the silvery curtains of mist. I could almost hear the whistling of ancient arrows. The atmosphere was lost on my brother, Thomas, who started pretending the castle was under attack.

"AAAAGGGGHHHH!" he screamed. "Close the drawbridge!" He'd had a lot of sugar on his Rice Krispies.

Suddenly, something caught my eye; something sparkling like a single star in a deep pool. It looked too new and precious to belong in the ruins of Corfe Castle. I walked over to it but, just as I reached it, I heard a noise – a melody. The music got louder and louder. As it did so, the mist thickened.

"Mum! Where are you?"

No answer. Just the mesmerising music, perhaps a flute or a harp. I moved forwards. Red, blue and green tents surrounded by congregating crowds lay before me. The drawbridge was open and flags were flapping like birds' wings.

Amazed, I walked into the castle. Suddenly, amidst the cheer, I heard moans almost drowned by the music. I followed the sounds, reaching a locked wooden door criss-crossed with heavy bars. Behind it, I could make out French accents – they sounded desperate. I pushed against the door but, to my surprise, I passed straight through it. Before me stood a group of thin men in hanging garments, their faces dull and grey.

"What's wrong?" I asked.

"No food for weeks." The man's voice was a scrape at the back of his throat. He seemed to look straight through me.

I must find the key.

I passed room after room until I found a room filled with books. Dust flew around the shelves like fairies. Tucked behind a dusty volume was a single key! I thought it might pass through my fingers but it was heavy in my hand.

I ran back to the dungeon, twisting the key in the lock until it clicked. The door opened and the men hobbled out.

I dropped the key in my hurry and while searching for it I noticed something shiny in the dungeon. The key? As I went to pick it up I heard my brother calling my name. "Come here! Look at this, Lilly!"

I was back in the ruins with Thomas in a room that looked surprisingly familiar.

The tour guide said, "King John used the castle to keep prisoners. He kept his daughter a prisoner and left twenty-two of her French knights to starve in the dungeon."

"But I let them go!"

"Pardon, dear?" The tour guide looked in my direction.

I did let them out, I did. Didn't I?

"Yes," whispered a scraping voice. I turned. Behind me, a group of frail shadows hobbled away from the castle. I blinked and they were gone. Were they actually real?

"Lilly?" my brother asked. "Who were those men?"

A Smuggler's Life
by
Sam

Today we were moving house, right into the heart of Lulworth. The car rolled down the steep and rocky hill. I could hear cows mooing in the fields. There were overgrown hedges spreading out over the road. Caravans were parked on the verges. Then I spotted a blanket of blue shivering in the breeze, surrounded by tall rugged towers of rock. The hedges peeled open to reveal a picture postcard cottage sitting boldly on top of the hill. This was our new home.

The removal lorry arrived, spilling out a wave of parcels which soon became an enormous pile inside the split stable door of the cottage. I took my belongings from the gigantic pile and rummaged around for my new red iPad. I quickly stumbled up to the attic for some peace. Once up the crooked and creaky ladder, I found myself in the dark musty attic full of silvery threads of cobweb. I slowly picked my way through the endless boxes and dusty furniture until I spied a small wooden box nestled in the corner. I blew off the dust, coughing as I breathed it in and peeled it open.

It contained only a small, dusty book. The title was 'A Smuggler's Life'. I tucked it under my arm and climbed back down the ladder and entered my new bedroom. My bed had already been assembled and I fell on to it, exhausted from the long day. I started to read the old book…

Lulworth Cove was eerily quiet, the sea a deathly black colour and the rocks hung over threatening every intruder. I saw a shimmer of light sparkle across the water and then I heard a faint paddle in the distance and a quiet splash of water spread across the cove. I could hear quiet mutterings and then I could make out a figure lifting a heavy object into a cave.

I started climbing down the rocky terrain towards them. Slowly and quietly I managed to creep closer and closer towards the cave until I could just see in. What I saw terrified me. There in front of me stood four old and rugged men with tatty shorts and leather waistcoats. The men were piling big bulky bags up against a wall; another man was drinking what looked like rum from a bottle.

I lost my footing on a rock; it made a loud clattering noise. The four men quickly turned around and shouted at me. I ran as fast as I could but one of them was chasing me. I was running up the tall cliff face, slipping on the rocks but slowly making progress. I turned around to see where he was and I could just see him climbing up behind me. He was gaining on me and was soon going to catch me. At that moment I heard, "You get down here!" I slipped and hit my head.

I woke to amazement. Had it been a dream? Then I saw my arms, bloody and bruised. Also some shells embedded in to my arm...

Not Traditional Burning
by
Heather Hayward

Seventeen-year-old Gwen stepped out of the wash house; she breathed in the air, relieved to get away from the heat of the copper and the steam. Her calf-length cotton dress was drenched in sweat from her morning's labour.

The weather was hot and stifling: mid-August 1948. The pungent smell of the furze bushes reached her nostrils as she gazed across the Common behind the cottage where she lived in Corfe Castle. Gwen worked in the village shop but on half-days she helped her mother who'd become more and more confused since her husband died.

Suddenly, Gwen saw a pall of smoke rise above the rooftops of Corfe Castle's houses, adjacent to the heath. Figures darted to and fro, beaters in hand, as they thumped down the fires erupting everywhere.

Traditionally, the furze was set on fire but this was the wrong time of year.

Her friend Ben yelled for her help as he sped past. The fire was out of control and every type of contraption was being used to put out the flames. Gwen's eyes stung; her thin-framed body struggled to wield the heavy beater that Ben had thrust in her hand.

She choked. A gap in the smoke revealed a figure she knew. More flames erupted. Shocked for a moment, until she realised the fire was heading towards Mrs Riley's cottage.

"Ben, we must go over there! Look!" she yelled.

Ben saw where she was pointing and fortunately others had also seen the encroaching flames devouring the furze in its path as it headed towards Mrs Riley's.

Gwen heard a loud bang.

"Oh good grief, she uses Calor Gas, don't she?" Gwen

yelled.

They could see Mrs Riley waving wildly at the window.

"She's trapped in her living room!" shouted one of the men.

Another bang.

Gwen did not hesitate. The cottages all had a similar layout. One door in, one door out. The Calor Gas container would be in the kitchen.

Beater in hand, she thrashed the flames; jumped the picket gate, oblivious to the risk she was taking. Reaching the door, she espied a bucket of water. Dropping her shawl in the water, oblivious to the water dripping everywhere, she wrenched Mrs Riley away from the window and half dragged, half pushed her out the door as she draped a shawl around the old woman's thin, shuddering shoulders.

Gwen was aware of being lifted high by someone before being hastily dropped away from the fires. Just in time, as a loud explosion sent flames shooting everywhere. The heat was intense.

Gwen struggled to her feet and ran on to the Common again. She had to find her mother. She guessed who had started the fire. She'd recognised her through the smoke earlier. The men found her where she had fallen.

Gwen couldn't hear the birds as they'd grown silent. Everywhere was silent.

"I reckon she's had a bit of concussion but she's coming round." Gwen didn't recognise the voice.

"You're home now, maid." Ben was leaning over her.

"Eee maid, you dos look better now." He grinned. "You did a fine job afore and I reckon you saved Mrs Riley's life with your quick thinking."

The doctor had advised him to tell Gwen the bad news later. Her mother was dead.

The Village Lost in Time
by
Ben

I always treasured our home. Mind you, I don't remember it well. I remember school rather well. Our teacher, Mrs Pritchard, would have things her way. At the time I was there, there were only nine of us in school. Standards were not going to slip in the eyes of Mrs Pritchard, though I now feel sorry for her. If the weather was bad sometimes there would only be five of us. You see, the journey meant that we had to walk through the farmers' fields.

I still remember, thirty years on, the feeling of the soft wheat brushing against our bare legs.

I remember the day that my mother said: "We're leaving."

The British Army would never regain my trust after that.

And that was that. We left. Never to return.

Until today.

Well, only I am returning. My mother was killed in the war a while ago. It's weird, isn't it? How much or how little something can change. Fortunately, Tyneham hadn't changed at all. Well, I say 'at all' but there were a few tiny changes. Why did I keep seeing signs saying *Tyneham: The village lost in time*? Reading one of the signs, I saw: *Tyneham Village was commandeered just before Christmas 1943.*

What?! This village; our village, was commandeered?

I ambled over to the schoolhouse. I saw houses; the old ones from Post Office Row. Well, houses may be somewhat exaggerating it. What were they? They were shells.

I found it vaguely funny: bullet shells make houses *into* shells.

And then, in a split-second, everything came back to me. Everything. Mrs Pritchard getting annoyed, and... I can't even get the words out. These were people's homes. This was my home.

Inside my raging body, something snapped. I slowly and silently slipped over to the information board. In one fluid movement I swept it aside. It seemed to fall to the ground in slow motion. All eyes were on my next movement. Why was no-one stopping me? But then, something much more unexpected happened. A woman threw the rope barrier.

"How yer doin'?"

"Helen!" I replied.

Everything came back to me. She and I were best friends back at school. We used to get a lot of stick for it: "Ooo! New girlfriend, eh?"

We got that every day. We didn't care.

Then came that fateful day when my mother said those unforgettable words.

I hadn't spoken to Helen in all these years.

And then an extremely old woman wheeled herself towards us.

"Little John Hecox!"

Was it? No, it couldn't be. Could it?

"Mrs Pritchard?"

"Yes, my dear! Gosh, look how big you've gotten!"

My head was buzzing so much. Mrs Pritchard must be, I don't know, eighty now? I hadn't seen Helen or her for thirty years. And yet, here they were.

And that is the story of how I met some very old friends by vandalising land owned by the British Army.

Kimmeridge
by
Jo Maycock

He could still feel her voice bruising the inside of his skull. Her words, sharp as butchers' knives, hacked and sliced away their past, dismantling all his hopes and expectations of a future together. Being with her was everything.

Standing in the doorway, his mind tangled into a knotted ball without an end or a beginning, he stood and watched the tail-lights of her car disappear into the night. Frozen, desolate, he wept silently as the seagulls screamed and swooped in the darkening sky. Turning back into the porch, blinded by tears, he stumbled into the basket that held their fossil collection, scattering the precious contents all over the floor. Angrily pulling on his boots, he swore and stamped on the pieces. Slamming the door behind him, he strode away from the cottage down the path that led to the beach.

The storm-battered village of Kimmeridge was at last settled and still, resting under a windswept sky as it welcomed the first stars. James strode down the lane muttering, "No, bloody NO! This isn't possible, she can't leave me, I won't allow it!"

The sea was just a distant murmur. He climbed the stile that led across the fields and around the hillside to the cliff edge and came to the wooden steps leading down to the beach. Something sharp jabbed at the sole of his foot, he pulled off the boot and tipped out a fossil. It was the one that they had argued about: she thought it might be part of a dinosaur, a tooth maybe, he had silenced and mocked her, dismissing the notion as nonsensical.

Holding up the fossil he said triumphantly, "She will be waiting for me on the beach, this is an omen, she couldn't leave me, she will be so sorry."

James put on his boot and, holding the fossil, raced down

to the beach, taking the steps two at a time. The weary sea tiptoed in and dribbled out over the black shiny rock. He stood, searching the emptiness, and howled: the sound bounced back with a growl and a deep-throated rumble, a rattling of cage doors. It deepened as he heard her voice saying, "I can't be with you any more, your rages scare me. I did love you once. I must go."

It was then that he had lashed out with his fists.

The cliff began to fall, peeling away from the crumbling face: great chunks of rock skied down to the shore, tumbling over and over. James ran to the steps and looking back, he saw a huge dinosaur, clear in the moonlight. Imprisoned for millions of years, it emerged from the falling debris, the backbone razor sharp, the great jaw full of massive teeth, the giant claws clinging on to the rock face.

James screamed out her name. The cliff answered by releasing the dinosaur. It crashed down, broken but free.

In the morning, James went to look for proof of the creature's existence. There was none.

The White Sail
by
Sophie

The blood red sun struck the sea with her venom, injecting it beneath the surface. The colour intensity rose, causing the crimson waters to start to seep towards the cove. Soon, the entire ocean as far as the eye could see, was dyed a deep red.

The woman's eyes caught the reflection and glowed.

Far out, the waves bubbled furiously, like water in a kettle; yet no warmth had penetrated the surface. The water took on the circular shape of the cove with its narrow bottle neck as it rippled towards the shore.

Her hair was whipped around by the wind; the smooth curls now tangled waves.

Perhaps on a summer's day, the rocks could be seen as inviting with their rounded tips home to all manner of creatures – oystercatchers, curlews, limpets – but not tonight. Their never-waning strength allowed them to pierce the cool surface, gleam proudly in the fading light.

Men's voices drifted loudly down the valley from the Lulworth Cove Inn, but the woman lay still. The day was coming to a close, and yet she'd never felt more alive: a witness to a spirited scene. The raucous sounds that spurted from the pub were drowned out by the boom and clap of waves against the sides of the cliffs beyond. The maroon light cast its colour on to the walls of the pale building.

Many a day had she lain in the golden light, on the jutting pebbles; you could not sit for long, only to see the sun dip her head below the horizon. The children would never stay still for they loved to explore the rocks, casting pebbles away. Maybe that's why they were taken, because they interfered with nature's course. The ocean worked tirelessly to return the stones to the shore, shifting them back and forth, only for them to be flung aside again by careless movements.

The sea battered the cliffs, targeting the cracks, the weakness of the stronghold. There was no set pattern to the limestone; some parts were silky smooth, other parts crumbling away.

She sat up, her papery skin succumbing to the harsh ground; the wrinkles seemed more defined as the eerie emission of light sought out the untouched crevices.

Finally, she cracked. In a frenzy, she began pelting pebbles at the advancing lines. The balance of power tilted towards her foe, but the barrage came crashing down. By the time they reached her, the legions lapped her toes. Shot after shot she fired, her regiment of anger tearing down all defences.

A white sail glided into the cove, and she stopped, puzzled by its serenity on the uncertain waters. Her exhaustion was sudden. She no longer felt the sharp stones she lay to rest on as the night had, at last, numbed her senses.

In time, the sun, her energy spent, took to her bed and gave way to the darkness.

Her eyes opened, all fire extinguished.

The wine transformed to ink.

EAST

The Last Bus Home
by
Penny Rogers

The crisp packet lodged around the toe of Teresa's shoe. She looked at it with distaste and tried to flick it away; there was so much litter and mess everywhere these days. In the end she had to plant her other foot on the packet to free it. The bus station was cold. A chilly wind whistled round her legs making the freezing bench even more uncomfortable. Teresa sighed. Only twenty minutes and she'd be on the last X6 of the day to West Moors. She prayed with silent fervour for a warm bus, adding an extra request for it to be clean.

Shifting on her uncomfortable seat she saw for the first time that she was not alone on the bench. A young man in a hoodie had perched on the end. He looked foreign. Teresa sniffed; there were people of every nationality in Poole these days. She pulled her coat tighter around her and ventured another glance towards the end of the bench. She didn't know the man but he seemed somehow familiar. Huddled against the cold in his scruffy trousers and inadequate jacket she saw in him the Piotrs, the Tomazs, the Jerzys that she had known as a child. She looked at him again, all the while pretending to be scanning the buses coming in. He saw her looking. She blushed.

"Where is that damn bus," she muttered just loud enough to try to cover her embarrassment. The man took a book out of his pocket and buried his head in it. With a start she saw that the book he was reading was in Polish, the language of her childhood.

She didn't notice the crisp packet blow back against her feet or even feel the cold any more. In her mind she was back in the Polish resettlement camp near Sherborne; her mum talking of a home in Poland that no longer existed and her dad trying to get work. She remembered playing with the other children, all born in north Dorset, oblivious to the tragedies that had brought their parents there.

At the other end of the bench the man stood up. He was so thin; he needed some good Polish food. Throwing caution to the now biting wind she forced two words out of her trembling mouth.

"*Dzien dobry.*" The effect on the young man was immediate. He spun round and stared at Teresa. "Hello," she said in English. "I hope you don't mind me speaking to you. It's just that I haven't spoken Polish for many years."

The X6 was there, almost ready to take her back to her snug bungalow. She considered the cost of a taxi, then looked at the tired face of the young man.

"Shall we go and find a cup of tea?" she asked.

The man said, "Please, you are very kind. My name is Piotr."

"I thought it might be," said Teresa. They shook hands as the bus pulled away.

A Cross to Bear
by
Claudette Evans

Violet rapped on the iron studded oak door, grasping Lily's hand tightly while they waited for the Master to let them in. The red-brick walls rose up before them and her heart sank, but they had no other choice. Following an examination by the doctor they were told to undress and bathe. Lily's hair was cut brutally short, then both were issued with the uniform: a coarse, grey dress, white mob cap and apron.

Discipline, they soon realised, was harsh, with the sexes being strictly segregated. Violet's daily drudge was picking oakum. Although she found this menial task both emotionally and physically draining, she was comforted by the fact that Lily was attending the local school. It might one day allow her daughter to escape from the harshness of life in the workhouse.

Had it really been only ten months earlier that Lily had stood with her mother on the crowded railway station, holding back the tears – trying to be brave – as both wished her father "Bon voyage"? In his uniform he looked even more handsome than the day they'd met on the bridge over the River Allen, near the Walford Water Works, where Alfred was employed as a stoker. Having a job of 'national importance' he would not usually have been conscripted, but being a man of strong principles, he'd felt duty bound to volunteer for Kitchener's Army.

Some six weeks later, answering a knock at the front door, Violet was handed a telegram by a boy in a Post Office uniform. She stood for some moments, then, undoing the envelope, read: *Missing – believed killed in action.*

Collapsing to her knees, Violet was beside herself with grief and was carried to her bed by the landlady. Lying there, she clutched their wedding photograph, sobbing uncontrollably, despairing for her and Lily's future. Most employers refused married women employment, so without a job, savings or supportive family, Violet was incapable of paying the rent on their small thatched cottage, adjoining the Beehive Inn. Being made homeless six months later, there was no real alternative other than entering the workhouse.

Peace was declared on 11th November 1918, but Violet, combing her prematurely grey hair, felt incapable of celebrating.

Christmas approached, seemingly without hope. Lily was working in the wash house, as was usual for the children on a Saturday, when she was summoned to Matron's office. Standing there was a skinny man in uniform, with his arm placed lovingly around her mother, and Lily, suddenly recognising her father, ran into his now outstretched arms.

Alfred returned to work at the water company and the family found lodgings in the Cornmarket, where one year later Lily was presented with a baby brother.

They often passed the workhouse and Beehive Inn, when strolling along the banks of the River Allen, but by the time Lily celebrated her sixtieth birthday, both buildings had been demolished. Only the bridge remained, the river beneath a symbol of their love.

Specto, Amo
by
Abigail

3586 days of working in security at the Dolphin Shopping
Centre. 3586 days of the boss looking over my shoulder,
constantly looking for the negative. 3586 days of the boss
shoving me this way and that way, flicking from camera to
camera to capture theft, violence and cruelty. Until recently
my cup was half empty, my life depressing and I felt as
though there was nothing good. In my time here I've seen
awful things; awful enough to make me want to leave it all
behind.

Until recently, despite the boss disagreeing and
muttering behind my back, I've witnessed goodness: an
angel. She owns the Grape Tree; I'll never know her name.
In the bleakness and cruelty, she glows in my eyes, a ring of
colour in the blackness. Thing is, she hasn't looked my way
and she never will. Why would she? She is innocent. Only
the wicked look at me, over their shoulder, as they plot their
devious plans. I once looked for the evil. That was my job; I
now look for her.

Over the past few months I've begun to feel she can save
me. I want to be with her, the angel. She is helping all those
around her, lighting up their lives. Every day she buys two
cups of coffee for the shivering people outside the front door
near her shop, people who have no homes. On her way to
lunch, she gives food to them too. She was late opening the
Grape Tree today because she was helping a man find his
car keys. She has performed many more small but important
miracles for others. If she can help them, then why can't she
help me?

Today there was an argument downstairs by the
escalator. He signalled me in its direction and straightened
up, eager to contact the police, poised to pounce on the

phone. As we watched I saw her, preoccupied in her shop with an elderly woman fumbling for her purse. Dreamily, my thoughts strayed to her and focused there instead. The boss shouted and screamed at me demanding that I stay focused on the real problem. He suddenly picked up the phone and dialled a number.

"The whole system is years old and it needs rebooting!" he exclaimed. "I try to move the camera but it's got a mind of its own!" His reply was in a lost language of mumbles. "Yes it's the security programme, Dolphin Centre, Poole." He continued, "Yes we can switch it off but not until the centre is closed for the day... OK, see you at six."

So I really am going to switch off. Once they reboot, I'll no longer be here.

My name is Specto 3000 and I am a security system that fell in love with a beautiful soul; an angel who helped others and will help more. I just won't be there to see it...

Old Man River Stour
by
Cilla Sparks

The bike rattles down the steep lane from Pamphill Green, past thatched cottages and the tiny shaded beer garden at The Vine pub. The sun is warm on her bare arms and the breeze on her face carries the scent and sounds of the river as she props her bike against the wooden gate at Eye Bridge. An ancient fording place, the river here is wide and shallow with a gentle weir and narrow wooden footbridge. Today the little car park is full; mums have brought their children, with after-school snacks, to play in the clear, cool water.

The Stour, timeless in the summer haze, rolls slowly down from Cowgrove, turning lazily towards the twin-towered minster at Wimborne, just visible behind the trees. She has always loved this place. She pictures it still so clearly, walking home downhill from the village school to paddle in the gentle lapping water, then following the path across the meadows along the river bank. The grass lush and long, brushing her scuffed school sandals, and the hedges promising blackberries to come; sparrows chattering in hawthorn bushes, and sometimes a glimpse of the still statue of a heron among the reeds.

The field path becomes a track as it approaches the riverside allotments, land gifted a century ago by old Mrs Hanham of Deans Court for the residents of Wimborne. She can still see her father bent over his spade, digging his beloved patch, as had his father before him. She hurries on in her mind, almost smelling the strawberries, red and sweet, warm and ripe for picking, hiding under shady leaves.

"Hello, my dear," her father turns in her dream, taller then and tanned, wiping his sweating brow with a dusty hand. "Pick some strawberries for our tea, my lovely."

She shivers as the sun clouds suddenly, dragging her back from her reverie to the present. Mounting her bike she cycles on, following the old pathway across the field, but not through the long grass of her childhood. The path is now asphalted, a cycle track, with carefully positioned benches overlooking the river. Newly planted trees and landscaped areas have opened up the views. Moorhens still bob along the river bank, but things have changed. The allotments are no more, no fruit to pick for tea. The cherished plots of generations have been cleared and developed; replaced with cul-de-sacs of new housing with paved front gardens. As she passes she feels again her father's pain the day he watched the bulldozing of his weathered shed, and the destruction of his strawberry beds.

She turns into a small courtyard of new retirement flats, stopping at number 6, Stour View Court. Lifting her shopping basket from her bike, she pushes open the door. The room is sunny, with bright French windows overlooking the river, and colourfully planted pots.

"Hello, my dear," she says as the little old man in his chair turns towards her. "Look, Dad. I've brought you strawberries for tea."

The Box
by
Ellis

Back then, before it all happened, I was just Jane. A fifteen-year-old ordinary schoolgirl from Poole, settling down to relish and enjoy the summer holidays.

After the first few days of my holiday I received a package through the post which I was expecting – after all, I'd just ordered some books from eBay. However, my parcel didn't contain any literature, only a box! A pretty, ornate, ancient-looking box! Of course there must have been a mistake, but there was a note attached that read:

Jane, look after this please. Trust no one.

Why me? My mind was racing with adrenaline and ebullience in the fact that this box might be something of importance. Why had it been sent to me? Well, it was all a bit odd really. Where were my books? I stood there, looking at the box which was lying so helplessly upon the kitchen table. I picked it up and scrutinized every inch of it. It was square – like most boxes. It didn't seem to have a lid but instead a pattern on the top. Several connecting triangles in a circle were ingrained in the oak.

I tried to move the shapes around, to get into it somehow, but it was no use whatsoever. I shook it about; not a sound. I put the box down, sipped at my cup of hot tea and stared straight ahead at the TV. It was just the Dorset news blaring from the screen, a newsreader speaking about an incident on a road in Bournemouth. I looked at the box. It stared back up at me like a lost child who has realised you're their only hope of getting back home.

I read the note a few times over. *Trust no one.* What's that supposed to mean? What's so special about this box anyway? Before I could finish my train of thought, I was interrupted by a sudden announcement on the news.

"Alexander Harris, the notorious professor of Natural History, was found dead at his home in Poole this morning. The death is being treated as suspicious and detectives are currently investigating. His house has been searched and it is believed a priceless artefact has been taken. If you have any information or have seen anything suspicious, please inform the authorities."

I sat down and put my head in my hands. What if this was the artefact? I looked back at the box. It was no longer an innocent child but a smirking devil. I pushed it away angrily. My heart pounded in my chest and my breathing quickened as I thought about all the possibilities ahead of me. Maybe I wasn't just an ordinary schoolgirl after all.

A Place of Her Own
by
Gail Chappell

Alison zipped up her jacket, put on her scarf and left the car park. She headed across the grass, drawn like a magnet to the top of the cliffs. She stood there, mesmerised, watching and listening as the tumultuous waves crashed against the deserted shoreline below, gobbling up the shingle beach. The wind was blowing directly into her face, taking her breath away, but she had never felt more alive. She turned and walked alongside the nature reserve, mindful of the tiny lizards scurrying across the sandy walkway. She strode purposefully towards the slope, relishing the challenge ahead.

The climb was invigorating, awakening every muscle in her legs as the incline became steeper, the path twisting and turning. Her heart was pumping, her head clear. No matter how many times she followed this path she felt the same excitement and anticipation as she approached the coastguard station at the top of the hill. She looked back briefly at the golden beach stretching behind her into the distance, but her focus was in the opposite direction.

She stopped and sat on a nearby seat. Wherever she went in the world she could never find a better view than this. Mudeford Spit. From the top of Hengistbury Head she looked at the curving coastline, dotted with rows of tiny beach huts, some facing the beach, others facing the little harbour, with Christchurch Priory in the distance. She sat there for a few minutes, and then began the slow descent to the beach, watching the empty land-train weaving its way along the narrow, winding road. She checked the keys in her pocket. The bumpy uneven steps were all that stood between her and her dream.

At the bottom she walked slowly along the beach,

remembering when she had run across the same stretch of sand as a child, shouting and laughing, racing to get into the water first. Happy family picnics on the sand, long sunny days and warm evenings; exhausted, but not wanting to go home to bed. She had returned years later with her own family, laden down with footballs, kites, surfboards and kayaks. They ate bacon rolls and hot dogs during those summers, cooked on a little camping stove in a friend's beach hut, before taking the ferry across to Mudeford Quay to go crabbing, having saved a few tiny morsels of bacon for their crab lines on the slipway, each determined to catch the biggest crab before returning home, tired but happy.

That was what she wanted for her grandchildren, and that was the reason she had bought Hut 248. She sat on the steps of the blue and white hut, with a flask of coffee, looking out across the sea and smiled. She had spent her entire inheritance on this beach hut. Everyone thought she was mad but she didn't care. Okay, so she didn't have any grandchildren yet, but when she did they would come and stay here too.

Ribbons
by
Ingrid Hayes

"Why, those trees go all the way up to heaven!"

Kathleen wished she shared Molly's optimism and handed over their last sixpence to the cart driver. They glanced up at the steamed windows of the laundry and made their way to the housekeeper's black door.

Before they reached the bell, they were startled by hurried footfalls. Flashes of blue-striped uniforms hovered at the side of them and questions darted across the air in urgent whispers:

"How old are ye?"

"Are yous walkin' out wiz someone?"

Before they could politely reply, the girls retreated swiftly and their attention was drawn to a figure on the steps before them. Framed harshly by the black door and her equally black dress, the housekeeper's face appeared phantom-like to the frightened girls. She began to recite a severe litany of instructions, which she concluded with a half wave in the direction of the laundry.

"She's mad!" Kathleen whispered.

"Well, at least it'll feel like home, then!"

They turned and retraced their steps back to the laundry. Kathleen opened the door and as they stepped into the hot, moist air the pounding of irons and rubbing on washboards ceased. An older woman stepped forward with reddened arms and glistening face:

"Are yous the de Lacy gals, come for the livin' in jobs?"

Kathleen and Molly shyly curtsied.

"Well I never. Wiz names like that we'll all be a curtsin' to yous! Meantime yous needs to be up afore daylight, no bed-buggin', mind! Sam 'ere will give yous a shout. 'Is job be getting coal in an' pinching ribbons off our Susan's 'air."

All the girls laughed heartily except a tiny girl with dolly-dyed arms who stared at Sam with watery eyes.

Kathleen and Molly were shown to the narrow staircase which led to their room above the laundry, but Kathleen let Molly go up first, resigned to disappointment. Molly threw their bags on the sagging bed. "Well at least it's big. Plenty of space for dancin'."

Kathleen surveyed the cold, windowless room. What could two fledglings from the Wicklow Mountains expect?

Kathleen cast a glance at her sister's forlorn eyes and in an instant knew that Molly's dreams were cut like ribbons. She surveyed the stained and browning wallpaper and saw a sliver of light above the chest of drawers. In an instant she clambered upon a rickety stool and fingered the unmistakable outline of a window. Carefully she peeled back the stiffened paper and called to her sister to take a look.

Peering down they looked upon landscaped gardens, which seemed to melt in the far distance to a vague horizon. Kathleen suddenly mimicked Molly's previous incredulity, "Why, those trees go all the way up to heaven!"

Drifting snowflakes swirled gracefully then fell to earth, littering the ground with fragments of ice. Kathleen looked at the thickening sky and could almost see their darting ribbons blissfully link above: free at last to roam and create dreams in the cold wintry air.

Grim Stranger Comes to Town
by
Becca

I sat down at the edge of the Minster Green on the crumbling stone wall. A steady stream of people passed me, all of them staring, none of them caring. My battered hat lay upturned by my feet, containing nothing but the ripped lining that gave away its age.

My fingers ached as I gripped my sign but I gritted my teeth and carried on through the pain. I needed the money.

Time passed and I gradually got used to the chimes of the church wanting to be heard every half hour. By now, the sun had slipped out of view and the wind started his nightly jog around the town.

I pushed my body (now heavy with fatigue) off the wall and stooped down to grab at the hat. My numb fingers brushed at the metal discs inside. I collected the coins and began to count. Three quid. Wasn't bad for a Sunday, I guess.

I normally hid my sign in the nearby foliage, but not tonight. It was colder and I could use it to block out the wind that tried to bite me in the night.

Sighing, I dragged myself and the sign to the bench outside the Quarterjack's sandwich shop and set up camp. I managed to jam my sign between the slats of the bench so that there was a right-angled triangle for me to lie through.

***

The usual blackbird wakes me up just as the sun rolls above the horizon. I stand and stretch, grimacing as my back clicks. I steal a glance at my reflection in the sandwich shop window. A boy: late teenage; a frayed navy beanie hiding floppy hair the colour of wet sand; hooded eyes that are aged beyond their years and creased, damp clothes that hang off my scrawny frame. I barely recognise myself.

I set off towards the Square. It's torture here later on – coffee-scented clouds drift over from Costa. But for now I can warm myself up in the sun's rays, waiting for nine o'clock to show up. Only then can I spend my three quid on food and drink. My stomach can't wait.

Nine o'clock. I am just about to make my way back towards Quarterjack's when I hear someone call my name.

"Tobias!"

I freeze. No-one knows my name. Not my real name. That can only mean one thing – he's finally found me. It's time to go. Only one thought crosses my mind as he beckons with a skeletal finger – I'll never have to beg again.

The White Lady of the Stour
by
Suzanne Webb

John Turner shivered as he turned up the heater in his van. Pulling out of the pub car park, he made his way home to the tiny village of Hampreston. He wouldn't have turned out at all on this bitter night had he not been in the darts team, but they relied on him.

He had to wait for the windscreen to defrost. It still wasn't fully clear as he approached Longham Bridge, but clear enough for him to see the woman in the white dress as she ran across the road. "Fancy being out without a coat on a night like this," John tutted.

As he drove across the bridge he was horrified to see the woman disappearing down the bank towards the river. Suddenly, her arms were flailing wildly, her white dress billowing like a sail. Screeching to a halt, he leapt from his van, crossed the road and slid down the frozen bank. She would surely drown!

Nearing the river he heard a strange sound from the bridge. It sounded like a horse and cart. Surely his ears were playing tricks? Glancing up he saw nothing. Nor could he see the woman.

John felt his heart banging against his chest, his body shaking. *Please God, don't let her drown!* Leaning forward to peer into the darkness under the bridge, he lost his footing. Moments later he was gasping, icy water filling his nose, mouth and lungs, and then blackness came... In the distance he could hear people chattering.

He opened his eyes to stark white light and a smiling nurse standing beside his bed. "You were lucky," she began, "you almost drowned. A passing driver saw you and rescued you. The police are waiting to have a word."

John accepted the offered cup of tea as a policeman and

policewoman entered the ward. Introducing themselves, they pulled up chairs, the policeman producing a notebook and pen.

"Good morning, sir," he began. "If you're feeling better we'd like to ask a few questions about last night?"

John began to relate his story, then asked, "The woman! Did she survive?"

"I'm sorry, sir, there wasn't anyone else."

John was bewildered. "But I saw her!"

"You're not a local man, then?"

John shook his head. The policeman looked at the policewoman.

"She almost claimed another one."

"What do you mean?" John asked.

The policewoman carefully explained, "A hundred years ago, on a stormy February night, a woman dressed in white had been walking on Longham Bridge when she was run over and killed by a pony and trap. Rumour has it that every February since, she has roamed the banks of the river Stour, trying to lure unsuspecting mortals to their death."

John gulped. She had almost succeeded. In future he would stay away from Longham Bridge on a winter's night!

'Til He Gets Back
by
Megan

I never knew what happened to my dad. He was there a few days after Mum was diagnosed with cancer. Then, one day he was by the front door with his bags packed, hugging me, telling me to stay safe and not to grow up 'til he was back. I realised what had happened when a small blue envelope with a typed front came through. I had seen a letter like this when Dad had written to me before. He never told me where he was, he always just told me that he was having fun and when he got back he was going to pay for Mum's treatment and we could all live happily ever after.

I ripped open the letter, I was so excited to hear from him. It had been three months since he went. I did not expect to be on the floor crying my eyes out, screaming for my mum. The words sliced through my head like knives: *killed in action*. Now I sit on Dad's tattered couch looking through the old photo album, remembering him. I look at the photo – me sitting on his shoulders when we were at the Moors Valley Country Park. I smile at the memory.

"Daaaaddy, stay still! I don't like it when you move," shrieks the four-year-old sat on the shoulders of her dad.

"Let me take a picture then," says the smiling mum behind the camera.

The dad and his girl jump around a bit too vigorously and the bridge jogs, throwing the mother into the water.

"This camera had better be waterproof!" she shouts.

I look at the next picture of him helping me pick a stuffed animal the day we went to the Moors Valley Country Park.

"What about the penguin?" he asked questioningly.

"No, Daddy, the penguin tried to steal my sandwich."

"Okay, how about the otter?"

"No, they make too many sounds for me to remember!"

"How about the fox?"

"Yes, yes, yes Daddy! He is a beautiful fox. I'm going to call him Kevin like you!"

"Silly!"

I walk up to my bedroom and look at the stuffed fox sitting on my bed, all old and with many holes from my too much love. I pick him up and hug him to my chest because I will never grow up, not 'til he returns.

For Better, For Worse
by
Sam Morley

Andy and Lisa were the perfect couple; everyone thought so. Within our circle of friends they were undoubtedly the best looking, most loving and popular – almost perfect. We were envious and resentful in equal measure.

When they announced they were getting married, it seemed only natural that it would be an amazing occasion. The invitations were stylish, location unique: it promised to be a truly fabulous day that would upstage all other weddings – especially my recent homespun, limited-budget affair.

Naturally when the day arrived, the sun sat in a cloudless sky. Why wouldn't it? The whole event was to be held in a marquee on Bournemouth's West Cliff beach, food supplied by award-winning caterers. The ceremony was tender and moving, with the gorgeous couple looking like the model of love. I couldn't stop a silent eye roll at their specially prepared vows: emotive and tender, making our conventional ones from *The Book of Common Prayer* seem trite and old fashioned.

After the ceremony we stood around sipping champagne and being professionally photographed, no favourite Uncle Bill taking *her* matrimonial photos. "Zero expense spared," Lisa giggled. "It's hopefully the only time I'll be doing this, so the photos must be perfect."

We took our seats for the breakfast and the happy couple joined us with Sister Sledge's 'We Are Family' blaring through the PA. When the starter was finished, Andy stood to make his speech. "Parents, family and good friends, I would like to thank you all for joining us on this momentous day of celebration. To my beautiful wife Lisa, thank you, darling, for agreeing to marry me: I'm sure you get more gorgeous every day."

This got a big "Aaah" from the crowd.

He coughed, and appeared to be a little flushed, as he continued, "I would also like to thank my best man, Roger. We have shared so much in our twenty years as friends, including the love of Lisa – as they have been sleeping together for the past ten months!"

There followed a stunned silence. "And," he continued, "for the doubters, under each of your chairs are some pictures of the happy couple." With that he dropped his speech, downed his champagne and walked out of the marquee.

Shouts erupted instantaneously as both families attacked each other. Their accusations and fighting spilled on to the beach. Romeo Roger tried to make a quick getaway but failed as he got walloped – straight on to Lisa's lap – by Andy's brother. She pushed him roughly on to the floor, screaming, "This is all your fault!"

Judging by the photos of the unlikely couple it would be only fair to say that the fault lay in a 50/50 position, along with many adventurous others, scattered like an erotic top trumps set across the tables.

I walked over to my husband and whispered into his ear with a wry smile, "Looks like Andy and Lisa weren't so perfect after all. Let's go home and be imperfect together."

Happy ever after.

WEST

Suspension
by
Jude Alderman

The moon waited in the sky above the chalk down. An ancient barrow was silhouetted on the brow of the hill. The study was a warm refuge. The writer, his balding head reflected in the glass of the window, answered no calls. He paused, put down his pen and breathed in as he considered the years that had passed.

The stranger had woken at dawn. The rain was silent as it hung in the air outside the bare room: sky breathing in and lifting. He was tired from his long train journey the day before, and his conscience troubled him. He washed. Dressed in the black clothes he wore for such occasions. Began the slow, thoughtful walk up the hill.

The woman hadn't slept at all. She had leaned against the bars of her window and breathed out. Breathed out all of it: the love and the fury and the grief. To any observer it would have looked like prayer. She also chose black: the figure-hugging, flattering silk dress she had bought to wear when she pretended to mourn her first husband.

Two women walked with her along the dark corridor: damp and cold, even though it was late summer. The sky blinded her for a moment as they passed out of the gates, the rain not falling, but suspended in the air. Pausing at the foot of the steps, she looked up at the man in black waiting for her, his abundant white beard like silence weighing across his chest. A heavy snowfall, a chill beauty.

The boy had also risen early, dust motes floating in a shaft of sunlight as he opened the cottage door. The walk across the heath, the summer morning a pale warmth on his skin. Rain barely felt as it drifted, not falling.

He joined the greedy crowd in the square, his fear hidden by the shadow from the high walls. Jostling. Waiting.

The sky held its breath for a moment as the town hall clock struck eight. Then the sudden drop. Falling through space but not reaching the ground, the woman in the black silk dress was turning slowly to the side, her face visible through the sodden black cloth over her head. A grotesque beauty, a fall from grace, a murderess with winged heels. The sky and the boy breathed out.

"I've done what had to be done," the man with the beard told himself. He came down the steps and walked towards the prison gates. A cloak of shadow swathed him. He would not come this way again.

The woman hanging. The boy staring. The pause in his thoughts as he tried to wrap his mind around the sight. The prison walls a barrier to understanding. The shadow over the summer morning.

The years hung heavy, then fell away, as the writer picked up his pen.

Truants
by
Madeline Goodey

The houses were not like the houses in my road. These houses were white. The front doors were painted in nice colours. I couldn't see any dogs or any people. I didn't want to call Pippa's name in case a bad person heard me and shouted at me for making a noise. I think a bad person stole Pippa because she won second prize in the dog show and that makes her valuable. People do steal dogs, especially valuable ones.

I'm safe in Poundbury. No-one knows me here and no-one asks me why I'm not at school.
This little kid came up to me babbling about a lost dog. He was on his own. He was shivering so I wrapped my scarf around his neck. He held my hand.

I saw a big girl at the end of the road. I ran and asked her if she had seen Pippa. She asked me why I was on my own and not at school. She put her scarf around my neck and held my hand. She said we could go to a café for hot chocolate.

The kid was way too young to be out on his own. I was scared when he held my hand in case someone thought I was kidnapping him. He said he was thirsty.

The big girl took me to a café. She told me to sit on the sofa in the corner. I wanted to lie down so I took off my shoes.

I had enough money for a hot chocolate. I tried not to look at the café man and kept my hat pulled down. I took the hot chocolate back to the kid. He was asleep. His shoes were off. He wasn't wearing socks. His feet looked red and sore.

The café man was cleaning the coffee machine, he was facing away from me. I left quietly. He didn't notice me go.

It was drizzling and getting dark. Too late I remembered my scarf. I hoped the café man would look after the kid.

September Cottage
by
Wendy Breckon

We arrived late. Missed the turning. Shops closed. Wind battering the coastline. Definitely not picture postcard.

"Lyme Regis is so iconic," said a close friend. "Remember the story of *The French Lieutenant's Woman* when we all fell in love with Jeremy Irons in the 1980s?"

The rain was lashing. Bouncing off the sea. Thunder and lightning lit up the Harbour Inn. People scuttled towards its shelter. There was a dark figure at the end of the Cobb. Probably the French Lieutenant looking for Meryl Streep. An altered ending. We both chuckled, wondering what John Fowles would have made of it.

September Cottage was up a narrow street on the right, in a long row. There was a shabby, blue door and an ancient sailing boat in the window.

"I'll try and park," my husband yelled.

I turned the key in the lock. A typical fisherman's cottage. Musty. A bit cramped. Stuffed full of the usual seaside paraphernalia. There were six church candles and a box of matches near the stove. I was lighting the last one when the lamps went out.

"Oh God... Thank goodness!" The room was icy. Shadows flickered on the antique bookshelves in front of me. Hopefully a short power cut. He would be back soon. I focused on a seaside painting.

Michael stumbled through the door. Wind howling. Dripping hair. Soggy black overcoat.

"Just had the strangest encounter," he said, throwing himself into a wingback chair. "This guy came out of the darkness, up a side street. Asked me if I knew of September Cottage. Couldn't see his face... no one else around."

"And?"

"I said no!"

"Why?"

"Got a feeling... Don't know..."

"Well, now you'll have to..."

"Yes."

Michael rushed outside. Peered up and down the narrow street. Picked up the wooden house sign made from an old paddle.

He turned the lock.

I pulled the heavy linen curtains.

We clung together like twisted driftwood floating at the sea edge.

"This is crazy."

"I don't like it."

"I won't sleep tonight."

Saturday morning was very calm. Lyme Bay a dull, murky blue. Fishing boats were moving out slowly to find their catch. Seagulls circling. I was fixing breakfast in the small galley kitchen.

"Well, look at this, Lydia!" Michael had picked up an old red book. "Purely random. Strange. Look what's inside. A local newspaper cutting from the 1980s."

"Murder at September Cottage on... 4th October 1989."

"4th October? 1989?"

"Twenty-five years ago."

"Today!"

"Young woman killed by spurned lover. Bernard Illot suffocated Harriet Glover because she married her childhood sweetheart George at..."

"9.30am."

We sat silently staring at the wall clock. Waiting for the hand to touch the bottom. There was another sound. A text. Neither of us moved. Michael's hand reached over and scrolled down.

'I thought you didn't know where September Cottage was?'

Footsteps crunched on the seaside pebbles. Three knocks on the shabby blue door. A deep voice through the letter box.

"Michael, aren't you going to answer...?"

First Visit to Bridport
by
Elizabeth Friend

Uncle held out my coat. "I am so pleased you and Susan are coming with me today. I need your help." Pointing at my teddy, he said, "I see she is wearing her best dress too."

I was four years old. It was to be a big adventure. We travelled from Salisbury to Bridport by bus, sitting upstairs in the front seats. I held my breath and squeezed Uncle's hand as we gazed at spectacular views.

"The sea, I can see the sea!"

"Isn't it wonderful! We will soon be there."

It was a long walk from the bus stop. We turned down a dusty track and there, opposite a farm and behind a huge wall, was the biggest house I'd ever seen. Uncle lifted me up in order to pull the bell rope. We waited. There were footsteps on a stone floor, then the door creaked open. A stern man stood in a dark hallway. He shook Uncle's hand and invited us in. He looked at me with a cross face, like my father's. I hid behind Uncle.

"May I introduce my niece, Elizabeth," he said in his big voice. Turning to me, using his soft voice, "I want you to have a good look around the house for me."

Clutching Susan, I skipped off to investigate. There were two massive rooms at the front; one with a glass bit added on. At the back was another large room, a pantry and a huge kitchen. A staircase led up to a half landing, where it split left and right. I found bedroom after bedroom, a bathroom and a toilet with a grand wooden seat. A further steep narrow staircase led to an attic. It was creepy there but I stood on tiptoes to see wonderful views across the fields to town.

As I made my way back towards the stairs, a man dressed in old-fashioned clothes was standing with his back to me. He took a watch from his waistcoat pocket and looked at the blank wall. I was about to say hello, when he turned away and walked up the east stairs, disappearing through a closed door.

"Did you see the man?" I called out.

"There's no one here but us," snapped the stern man.

"Where did you see him?" asked Uncle.

"Half-way up the stairs. He was looking at the wall, as though there was a clock."

"Oh," he replied. "That would be a splendid place for Grandfather's pendulum."

The stern man asked him if he'd made a decision.

Crouching down, Uncle whispered in my ear. "Would you be very kind and ask Susan Bear if she thinks this would be a good place for me to live?"

I asked her, then announced, "Susan thinks it would be just perfect."

Turning to the stern man, Uncle said, "Very well, then I shall delighted to become the vicar of Allington."

Reverend A.L. Luker
Vicar of St Swithun's Bridport 1955 – 1963

The Old Man on the Hill
by
Thomas Beauchamp

Crisp sun pierced through the chill frost sparkling around my feet. Birdsong echoed through the hills celebrating the joy of dawn. Down below, pools of ethereal mist clung to the shadows as morning's warmth crept its way up the valley.

As I had done every morning for many years, I surveyed my village, the inhabitants slowly rising. There, I thought to myself, is Mr Hays the shopkeeper, laying out his wares for the busy day ahead. And there is Dr Martin rushing off to work.

Across the valley Miss Smith was tending to her sheep. She had been up before sunrise, and no doubt would work long past sunset. She often looked out and saw me, standing on the hill. Oh the stories you could tell, old man, she mused.

Mr and Mrs Andrews were out early walking their dog, "Good morning, sir! Glad to see you looking well." I smiled, pleased to see my villagers so happy. They were married on this hill three summers back. Oh, there was dancing and merriment that day! I had not seen such dancing for years. Back when I was young, people would sing and dance and feast upon these hills. But now that fun was long forgotten, kept only in the minds of those old enough to remember.

Time seems to run faster these days. Everyone is in such a rush, driving cars and texting each other. I was born to an age when the people of this valley would work the land with their hands, and where the nearest town was a day's walk away. I remember the village youth playing in these fields, and learning in the village schoolhouse. People would live, love and die in this valley. I remember too the old abbot who used to live in the village. He was a jolly fellow, always there to look after those in need. Alas, even the abbey had been forgotten, turned into private housing for the rich.

As the day wore on Dr Martin always took a break to come and visit me. She was a kindly sort; she would tell me about her day, the amusing patients she had had, and how her family was doing.

"You are looking very scruffy today, old man," she remarked. It was true; it had been a while since the kindly people who look after me last visited. "Here, let me help you." She took out her scissors and carefully trimmed away the worst of the tufts growing on my face, and brushed off some of the dirt from my shoulders. "Look there," she said, pointing down into the valley. "You have visitors!"

In the car park across from where I stood a car pulled up and out jumped a father and son. I recognised the father; as a boy he had lived here in my village. "Who's that, Daddy?" asked the boy.

"That's the Cerne Giant, son, the old man on the hill."

On the Rocks
by
Maya Pieris

The bike fell silent. She removed the helmet, the wind
making her gasp, whipping back her hair. Golden snakes
he'd called them. She inhaled sharp, salty fresh air, sitting
motionless before the horizon – Portland to Lyme and
beyond. Dismounting she realised how an old dog might
feel trying to pee and balance. Now she creaked more than
the leathers – his leathers.

They'd loved it here, since the first visit over thirty years
ago. Patrick – tall, blonde, elegantly handsome, who'd
shown her how to make whiskey sours, carved absurdly
large sculptures, played guitar well enough to have earned a
fortune.

"No, like this. Ice into jug, a good measure of JD – that
won't drown a fly – those lemons. Cut in half, squeeze, bit of
sugar. Press the button – go on. It won't bite. Perfect – ice not
too slushy. Don't want 'day after snow'! Mugs'll do."

It was still her favourite drink. Patrick who'd turned up
with a helmet he'd said would fit. "Never been on a
motorbike? Dangerous? What isn't?" And driven her
stylishly but safely here.

Hadn't been the Jurassic Coast then – just Dorset, a
backwater not backdrop to film and TV or fodder for
documentaries on coastal erosion, the joys of cream teas.
They'd parked up by a fish and chips hut, shared a double
portion, drank canned beers, taking in the hugeness before
them – scenery and life. Then started living together within
weeks of that first whiskey sour, ditching long-term
partners.

He'd bought a ring. "More pebble than rock," and
grinned. No-one had expected it would last, that obsessive,
self-absorbed Patrick would be such a natural father. He'd

been better with the kids than her. They'd gravitated to his hands-free approach like fish to water. And they'd all loved the water here – the emerald greens, blues of summer; slate greys of winter and all the colours between. So they'd moved here keeping a bolt-hole in London for their urban fix, the journeys often made on the bikes, latterly built more for comfort than speed.

Then, "We're on the rocks," he'd said handing her the whiskey, soured, and life fractured, crushed like the ice in her glass. And she hadn't known this man, seduced by the fresher charms of a girl – so bloody predictable, embarrassing. She'd felt winded and stung by his explanation as she did by the wind around her now, seemed to barely know herself. Or realise that if love is deep so is hate and as sudden and intoxicating.

He'd been found on the rocks just below here, a tragic accident, the verdict. A place known for its unstable terrain. The press coverage was generous – the loss of one of Brit Art's finest, though one wag commented: "Some thought he'd been washed up for some time."

She turned to face inland, decision made – *her dream*. An art school for anyone wanting answers through paper, paints, pens and stone. And she was going to build it here; call it 'On the Rocks'.

Dating at St Catherine's
by
Karen Wright

Jake snorted as he read the information board for St
Catherine's Chapel. Apparently it was where young women,
wishing to marry, came to say a prayer to find a husband.
Mind you, Net Partner's 100% guarantee to find your perfect
match hadn't exactly come up trumps either. Suki was
undeniably glamorous and the sex had been, well,
adventurous, but sadly after three dates, an unguarded text
message had revealed what his friends had been warning
him of. A visa, and not happily ever after, had been
uppermost in her mind.

He had come here to clear his head. The wind was
certainly doing that. He zipped his parka right up to his
neck and pulled the hood up. He was nearly at the top of the
track now, the ancient ridges of the hill curling away from
him, and eventually giving way to the shingle slopes of
Chesil Bank and The Fleet, a long gleaming ribbon of
trapped water, punctuated by swans and wildfowl. His
flapping Landranger map told him that it was the Isle of
Portland looming out of the mist on the horizon. He took out
his new digital camera; he would get some good shots here.

The sun came out as he was putting it away.

"Damn!" The sky was transformed, the sea glinting
aquamarine instead of a fitful grey and silver, the dour
chapel now a honeycomb yellow.

Glancing at his watch, Jake decided he had time to look in
the chapel. It was empty, apart from an eccentric looking girl
with a sketchpad. Strangely, it seemed much smaller from
within. From the coast road it was the dominating feature in
the landscape, but inside he doubted if there would be room
for more than thirty celebrants. The building had the air of
being long neglected, its back windows boarded, and large

limey puddles on the floor. By the doorway he located the kneeling hole for those wanting to pray for spouses.

"What about those of us looking for wives?" he muttered.

The girl gave him a knowing smile. Embarrassed, he looked away, tried to adjust his camera, and attempted a few interior angles. Then, as he packed away, he managed to drop his lens cap.

"Here, I've got a clean cloth if it's any help?"

"Er, thanks." He stepped towards her to take it shyly. "That's an um, interesting sketch."

God, he was out of practise! Actually the perspective was terrible, and why had she drawn a wheel in one corner?

"Do you really think so? I was about to give up."

She took off her bobble hat and her long auburn hair cascaded down over her shoulders. She shook it out, then turned to Jake, her pale, rose-tinted skin catching the light. Extending her slim, pastel covered hand she said, "I'm Catherine, by the way."

Yes, I can do traditional, thought Jake, as he clasped her hand in his.

The Hangman's Cottage
by
Alan Whittle

There wasn't much laughter in the Hangman's Cottage – not like last night.

Last night, the whiskey had flowed. Mrs Collins, the caretaker, had excelled herself. There had been great big doorsteps of bread and butter, a Stilton cheese and an enormous pork pie. Young Thom Pierrepoint, the hangman's assistant, had treated the company to several lugubrious Irish ballads.

Then this morning, the execution. This time Gregory Belfield – just eighteen years old – from down the Piddle Valley. It was his first Saturday night in the pubs of Dorchester. His first sniff of the barmaid's apron. And fists had flown and blood had flowed, then somehow a dagger had found its way into the heart of a peddler man.

Tonight the two hangmen sat in sullen silence, chain-smoking cigarettes as Mrs Collins served them cups of tea. Finally, Thom said, "I'm off to have a drink down the High Street."

"Watch your back!" counselled his mentor, a man with deft, merciless fingers and unfathomable competence.

The knock on the door came twenty minutes later. Mrs Collins ushered in Dan Belfield, younger brother of the man executed this morning. He was lighter and sprightlier than his brother. Out of professional habit, the hangman reckoned he would need another sixteen inches drop.

The boy started speaking. "He wor right upset, it broke his mam's heart to see him there... He were cryin' an' goin' at it somethin' pitiful, that's what she said..."

The older man said, "Well of course Gregory was upset... His mother seeing him in such a remorseful situation."

He spoke deferentially, choosing long words like

'remorseful' and 'situation' to calm this bumpkin down. "But you know, not long after your mater left, the Padre had some kind words for him. Gregory calmed down an awful lot. He was reconciled. I fought in the Crimee, and I never saw any soldier face death so calmly as did your brother Gregory this morning."

They were quiet for a second, then the hangman said, "You got something for me, boy, I believe?"

The boy hesitated before handing over two golden sovereigns. "You did do that thing to help him out?"

"Of course. It was over in a flash for him. I doubt he felt a thing. Against regulations of course. I could lose my job, but I did what I could to ease his passage to salvation. Would you like a cup of tea before you walk back to Piddletrenthide?"

Pierrepoint reeled into the cottage an hour later to be greeted with a whiskey-sodden cry of jubilation.

"I got five shillin' for you, boy!" the older man shouted. "The lad came up with a pound to ease his brother's passage to heaven..."

Thom smirked back at his boss, before asking, "What *did* you tell him?"

"Just the usual rubbish."

Pierrepoint started softly singing a ballad: a piteous tale of a young Irish patriot bound for the high gallows tree.

Spontaneous Sunday Seagulls
by
Lisa Dixon

Sunday afternoon, I'm struggling to keep up my momentum to train for this half marathon!

My iPod has given up on me... I have given up on me!

I decide to slow down and walk for a while.

The sun is glistening and the waves are crashing! Wow! Weymouth is so beautiful!

Seagulls above me are soaring with ease, a strong wind blows, but the seagulls seem to go with it, happy to be guided by the powerful blasts. Did they know the wind was going to be so strong today? Were they excited to be riding the gusts? Are they looking for food or just having fun?

I continue to watch, gazing in awe at my beautiful surroundings, and these, usually horrid creatures, so gracefully dancing in front of me.

Suddenly, the beautiful, gliding creature I was dreamily gazing at, turns and drops to the ground, as quick as if you or I had just realised we had forgotten to turn the iron off before we had left the house!

It picks up a shell, darts up into the air, before letting the shell fall to the ground. Smash!

Ahhh! That was its plan all along; in my mind this seagull was playing in the wind and enjoying this wonderful Sunday. But the seagull had me fooled, along with its prey: his spontaneous soaring was with purpose!

With that in mind, food sounded like a good plan to me too!

The Soldier in the Woods
by
Simon Leighton

Two hours on the road and I'm cursing the pint of water I sank on my way out. It's only ten minutes away, but I'm busting. Thankfully this part of the world has plenty of laybys and country lanes; with the sunlight fading I should be able to stop any old place.

She's waited ten months, she can wait another few minutes. The thought stabs at me. It's taken me ten months?

Here's a good spot; Cuckoo Lane, off the A35 and plenty of trees. Reckon I'm a bit cuckoo sometimes. Then again, who wouldn't be, the things I'd... never mind.

I swing in and stop suddenly, bit of a skid. These thoughts are making me jumpy. Afghanistan will do that to you, although that's not what's bothering me today.

'She's yours', the letter had said. Don't remember much else than that. That was the highlight, if you can call it that.

I step quickly from the car, it's cold and the wet grass squelches underfoot. I head for the nearby wood; the cover of trees is only polite.

Leaning against the first solid tree I spatter the leaves at my feet. Thank god!

A moment's relief passes and I find myself staring at a strangely familiar sight. I know this place. It's Thorncombe Woods. I came here on exercise back in my training days, must be twenty years ago now. Gloom has taken over, it's enveloping, encroaching on me, and as much as I stare in through the trees, the darkness leers straight back.

A pleading coo of a wood pigeon echoes about me, the leaves above crackling under a forceful blow of wind. I feel the need to walk further in, like I'm going to capture some nostalgic glimpse of my youth. Certainly I'm getting a good lungful of nostalgia from the rotting vegetation crumpling under my boots as I go, throwing up whiffs of musk and mould with each heavy step.

There's an abrupt chill. I turn and something's there. It can't be… hovering? It is! It's floating around a metre above the ground, dressed in Roman armour but somehow translucent. We make eye contact. I'd have expected to feel fear, but instead, looking at this thing as one soldier to another, there's guilt. *He knows.*

Suddenly squinting his ghostly eyes, his pale face falls and oozes into a stretched terrible writhe of white mist, his spirit spiralling over the dead leaves towards me with a ghastly wail. I try to shout but I'm muted by terror. My legs cave and I'm forced to claw at the ground like an animal as I flee. I can see the car, I'm pulling myself closer to it through the dank mud, scuffing my knuckles on broken twigs and bark as I scuttle for my life. I risk a look back, it's gone.

Falling back against the grass verge, I slide down, and sob. *I'm sorry.*

On Golden Cap
by
Sharon Beauchamp

The view from Golden Cap is always worth the climb. The path marked out by hundreds of footsteps before, lures you through abundant hedges, across luscious green pastures and along the coast path to a stunning sandstone summit.

It doesn't feel like twenty years since the first time my son and I walked together along this route. Although the landscape remains the same, we absorb more of the surroundings each time. Our dog once unwittingly disturbed an adder who was warming its diamond back in the early spring sun. It afforded us only a glimmering glimpse of his beauty before shyly slithering away.

There was always something to notice: birds, butterflies and occasionally beef. Negotiating the hulking presence of these ruminating beasts when they laid their massive chestnut bodies across our path required some determined courage. These docile brutes looked as though they had been in that cattle field since the time of Thomas Hardy, when perhaps he had noted them as rich threads in the fabric of his Dorset.

My boy was a tender four years old when we first embarked on this route. Over breakfast we had consulted our map seeking a footpath to the highest point along the coast. Our week camping in Charmouth was meant to be a beach, ice cream and sand-in-the-picnic type of holiday. Instead, it proved life changing.

We set out slowly, I held his hand and we sang songs. His little legs needed frequent rests so we stopped often, taking in the views. I never really thought we'd make it all way to the Cap but we were having a lovely day trying.

We forged ahead, both tired and hot till finally after the steepest climb, we found ourselves at the top. The air was clear and the sunlight was strong and bright, catching the blue expanse of Lyme Bay. It was spectacular. We sat and listened to the sea, the birds; and the puff of achievement as one or two others made it to the pinnacle. The crystal clear brightness of the place gave a pinpoint focus to my thoughts; I looked at my boy and knew Dorset was where we belonged.

Just as reaching the top was a process that needed some planning and changed depending on the variables and influences of the moment, the journey to Dorset would take years of working through for the whole family: finding jobs, changing schools and buying and selling houses. Like the landscape, the vision was always the same and we managed and adapted to the challenges along the way.

After some years now in Dorset we are settled. We feel we notice all that is around us with a sense of belonging, understanding the rhythms and cycles of this place as though it breathed itself.

The path to Golden Cap is, as always, invitingly familiar although always somehow different; now it's my legs that need to stop to rest and my son will take my hand to help me along the way.

A Bit of a Story
by
Wendy Breckon

The Jurassic Coaster was late. Excessive traffic in
Weymouth. Roadworks in Chideock. The usual bottle-neck
outside Lyme Regis.

Jim noticed a young woman with red curls standing next
to him.

"Is this one free?"

He sighed. Time to move the carrier bag. Someone
needed the seat. No chance now to gaze out of the
window. Admire the Dorset landscape. She might engage in
lively conversation. Amazing what some strangers told you
in a short time. Often they turned up the next day in your
favourite haunt – with the person they wanted to throttle.

"Here for long?" Her eyes focused on the carrier bag
wedged beneath his feet.

"No... Just a day trip. You?"

"Visiting my aunt..."

The delayed bus arrived at the clock tower. The back row
cheered, as if the pilot had made a successful landing. Jim's
young companion jumped up carrying her bunch of white
lilies. He would wait. A mad scramble for the front.
Everyone wanting to be first. He anchored the carrier bag
between his knees.

"Have a good day."

"You too."

Jim had forgotten to introduce himself or ask her name.
His thoughts had been elsewhere. Never mind. More
important now to plan the next step... Maybe a cup of tea at
the Harbour Inn. Fish and chips on the sea wall fighting off
those pesky seagulls. Perhaps a moment to dip a toe in the
water.

Jim stepped out into the Lyme Regis haze, feeling slightly

conspicuous with his green carrier bag. Marine Parade was teeming. August Bank Holiday. He was simply... one person lost... in a crowd. Must keep walking. Soon be there. The piece of paper was still in his back pocket.

An ambulance was parked at the far end... near the harbour. A blue light beaming on the Cobb. People were pushing closer, wanting to help. A figure lay on the beach. Paramedics close by. Jim became curious. A moment of distraction. A slight detour. He would only be a few minutes late. He strolled across the crowded sand, dazzled by the bright sunshine.

"Oh..."

"She just collapsed."

"Very suddenly."

"Maybe the heat."

"Hope she'll be OK."

"That's her niece over there, with the curly, red hair."

"She looks so..."

"Poor thing."

Jim squeezed briskly between the two people. Perhaps he could offer some comfort. A shoulder to cry on.

"Hello... I'm so sorry... er?"

"Rose."

"Jim Matthews, the man on the bus... Is this your...?"

"Yes." Her hands were trembling. The flowers lay on the sand. "I think it's too late... they're doing their best. Must have gone for a stroll. Now I might never see Aunt Sadie again. She had something to tell me. Someone she wanted me to meet. Y'know, a tale from her past."

"Yes, I understand. Sadie Leighton... Can't quite believe... after all these years," he murmured. "Dear Sadie, sorry I missed you..." He placed the carrier bag in the young woman's hands.

"For you, Rose," he whispered. "It's time you knew our story."

Ghosts of Max Gate
by
Elizabeth Thomas

Leaves have drifted into the angles of the house – death traps. I scoop them into the wheelbarrow: the colours of autumn, the colours of fire, even before I have set a match to them.

Early morning mists are wreathing the fields towards Stinsford. It is time to re-awaken the ghosts. A slow burning as flames lick, savour, sigh, take hold. Tendrils of grey smoke rise up, dance a little, swaying to the rhythm of the season, then fade into the frosty air. It is All Souls' Day and the long-departed are restless. Memories stir.

Although 'tis nigh on forty years since my mistress passed on, I can still hear her voice calling, "Mind to check for hedge-pigs, Job, before you start your bonfire. They are God's creatures."

The smoke thickens, moves sluggishly. I cannot look away. Her face is there as plain as can be, pleading, crying, "Never forget me, Job."

I reply, "I promise I never will." I see the steam from my breath mingle with the smoke.

***

After the mistress passed away, nothing was the same again. The master's new wife was a very different kettle of fish. I would much rather forget her but she haunts me too, her and her destructive ways. One day stands out above all others, the day she burnt my mistress's diaries.

"Throw these books on the bonfire!" Her shrill voice splintered the calm and rooks rose from the Scots pine in loud protest. I pulled the pages of script from their bindings and fed them to the pyre. To Miss High-Almighty I was just the gardener's boy. Never occurred to her that I could read and write and had feelings. Nor that I was fond of old Mrs Hardy. I'd probably have got the sack if that new Mrs Hardy had had her way.

Late that long-ago day, the ashes grew cold and blackened. As I trudged down the driveway to go home for tea, I turned and looked back. The master was standing by the scorched ground, his head bowed, a small, pathetic figure. About midnight, when bats circled the turrets, I felt compelled to rise from my bed and return to the wood-smoked garden. I stood in the shadows of the trees and looked up at the house. The master was standing at his study window. As I watched, a large moth fluttered in, drawn to the oil lamp. He darted to its rescue, catching it in cupped hands. Tenderly he released it into the night. He closed the window, the lamp went out and the ghosts of Max Gate were still again.

***

The fire has died down, all passion spent. The Scots pine whispers its secrets to the night and it is time for me to go home.

Easter on Colmer's Hill
by
Karen Wright

There were families scrambling up ahead of them. Snatches of laughter and cries of excitement blew back. Someone's red scarf was carried off, eventually snagging on a crooked arm branch.

Joe tugged Mimm's hand. "Come on! We've got to get a big one."

From the schoolyard, where they had registered, the hill had looked marzipan smooth, with an easy climb to the tree-tufted crest. From this side on, however, the steep dome seemed to rise almost vertically, punctuated only by jagged gorse and stiff brown brackens. For a six-year-old, whose wellies were already rubbing, 'challenging' was probably the appropriate Mumsnet phrase to use.

The late morning sun was slanting across the fields behind them, bathing everything in shades of honey and caramel. It made Mimm feel warmer, even though her hands were starting to throb. Joe was soon successful, lunging triumphantly at the golf tee that guaranteed a small egg, but kneeling absentmindedly to examine it, right in a pile of sheep poo.

Mimm wished she could divert her thoughts so easily. She glanced at her mobile again, although she could clearly recall the text: 'I can't come back until I know that there's at least a chance that you'll forgive me'.

"Never mind," said Mimm, swatting the worst off.

After a lengthy side-stepping, crawling ascent, they had found three more.

"But what about the Lucky Clovers?" wailed Joe, hot tears rolling over his screwed up cheeks. "And my feet hurt!"

"Well, there are only five to find on the whole hill."

"I WANT A BIG EGG!"

"Hey!" Mimm scrabbled around in her deep pockets for a tissue. "Let's sit down for a bit. I bet you can't see the sea from here."

"Yes I can," sniffed Joe.

Mimm tried to ignore that shifting feeling in her tummy that she got looking out from the hill, where the earth falls away, and the sky and the fields fill your vision. She and Joe were only a very small part of this evolving landscape.

"Come on, we need to go home for lunch."

"But what about the…"

"We'll look on the way back down, OK?"

Joe's lip wobbled, but he started off, holding Mimm's hand tightly.

As they reached the thick grass tussocks at the bottom of the hill, Joe stumbled and nearly fell.

"LOOK! Cor! Can I touch it?"

"No! Well… I suppose so." Mimm couldn't help recoiling. The sheep gawped whitely at them, its black eye sockets regarding them mutely. Jack moved forward slowly, fascinated. Reaching out he picked up the skull and what remained of the jaw-bone and teeth.

"Is Daddy dead too?"

"No! No! He's coming back to us." As Mimm heard herself, she realised with a jolt that this was what she wanted too. To begin again: yes she could do that.

"Let's collect our cream egg shall we?"

"No, it's OK," Joe clutched the skull to him. "I don't need one now."

D-Day Landings
by
Marion Cox

"It's getting late, Vera, we'd better go."

In Portesham village hall, Sheila glanced at her friend, neatly dressed in headscarf, skirt and cardigan instead of the rough jacket and farmyard trousers she usually wore. Vera, a farmer's daughter, was never normally seen wearing a skirt except on Sundays.

"What did you think of this lot of soldiers tonight, eh?" Sheila said, smiling as she thought of the burly American GI servicemen who that evening had crowded into the hall for refreshments. Such an assortment they were, big, loud and friendly, offering to get nylon stockings for the girls and handing out chewing gum.

For this quiet rural Dorset community, the arrival of GI soldiers preparing to cross the English Channel was a new experience, even in wartime. Of course the villagers knew what Americans looked like – they had seen them on screen at the cinema in Weymouth – but as the men lined up in the hall for cups of milky tea, it was exciting to hear in real life the exotic accents they usually associated with handsome film stars.

"Those soldiers have really cheered up the war, I love them," Sheila said with a grin. "One of them has promised to get me some bananas and tinned peaches, what a treat!"

Vera picked up her handbag and buttoned up her cardigan.

"And how are you going to pay him for these treats? I bet he'll ask for more than a friendly hug," she said. "Come on, turn off the hall lights before I open the door, we don't want to get into trouble for ignoring blackout regulations," she said.

The friends made their way outside where clouds had

turned the rural landscape into impenetrable darkness. As they parted company, Vera switched on her torch, its dim glow just reaching the path beneath her feet.

Her long walk back to the farm was along a quiet country lane that rarely saw traffic other than the occasional farm vehicle. As she strode homewards, she thought she heard a footstep behind her and though doubting there could be anyone there, she quickened her pace.

The footsteps followed. Her heart pumped with fear. The American GIs stationed in the village were big and strong and one of them might easily attack her. Vera hurried on but the footsteps hurried too.

Suddenly a man's voice spoke out and she half-turned to see the buttons of an American army uniform glint in her torchlight. Vera gasped and let out a muted cry.

"Hey lady, you sure can run fast," said a soft brown voice. "I've been trying to catch up with you. You need someone to walk you back home on a lonely road like this. Let me go with you."

Vera shone the torch into the soldier's broad and gentle face. He smiled.

"You will be quite safe with me," he said reassuringly.

Instinctively knowing that she could trust him, Vera returned his smile, took the GI's arm and they made their way along the lane together.

Changes in Pageant Gardens
by
Natalya

The girls trickled into Pageant Gardens like honey glooping through an opening. They collected around a small ancient sign; its edges were worn and rusty from shoulders that had brushed past it without noticing – as indeed the girls would have done had their teacher not dragged their attention towards it. She was a stout woman with dyed-red hair – some might even call it crimson – and it closely matched her character. She was extravagant, energetic and, above all, she was passionate about her subject.

Her effervescent nature was sometimes too much for her students who tried to counteract her enthusiasm by having a permanently bored look on their faces. They sulked and grumped in groups. Shoulders slumped and weight tipped on to one leg, they watched without interest as their teacher flapped her hands with enthusiasm.

The girls whispered among themselves and a couple sniggered about a loose strand of hair which was now dangling over the teacher's eye. The teacher, however, did not notice as she was so caught up in describing the legacy of the Digby family and the Pageant Parade which happened right where they were standing.

"...The band would play, there would be sweets and dancing and festival games..." She paused for breath, "then all the children would perform a song..."

But despite her best efforts, she could not engage the girls in this description. They were looking around, not for inspiration but rather to find a way of daydreaming which was so effective they wouldn't hear the constant buzz of the poor teacher who had now begun to recreate a dance that, "Everyone knew back then."

The sun ducked behind one of the clouds and suddenly

the golden glow turned a grey blur. The new, fresh leaves of spring rustled in the wind making the pretty dappled pattern into a matt paste on the ground. The girls carried on sulking and the teacher carried on talking as the weather steadily deteriorated.

Soon clouds covered the entire sky and droplets of rain scattered over the surroundings. The teacher's hair stuck like the tentacles of an octopus over her eyes. Reluctantly she acknowledged that the opportunity for her inspiration had died along with the good weather and that it was now time to leave the tour of Sherborne. The weather had killed any chance the girls had of being inspired, so slowly they dragged themselves back to the house.

Had they been looking closely they might have noticed the rain trickling down windowpanes or sitting in puddles on the worn benches. Had they been inspired they might have listened to their teacher and have seen how much the landscape changed with the weather. But they weren't, so they didn't and instead trudged back to school to lock themselves away in their rooms; the rooms which didn't change with the weather – they only changed when they wanted them to.

Still Falling
by
Britta Eckhardt-Potter

It was the Easter weekend and you were fed up with sitting around inside and watching TV, so we decided to take a drive to Portland and walk around the quarry. It was a fairly warm day and the air was fresh and full of new beginnings. We both had been through a tough time. You supported me through my father's death, clearing out the place I called home and trying to get settled in my new surroundings. Now it was spring and a good time to find myself again.

We parked on top of the hill and walked towards the quarry. You were walking too fast, as usual, whilst I was trying to take photographs. As we entered Tout quarry from the south there were already quite a few sculptures. I was impressed, started taking pictures of almost every one. I was so completely lost in photography and my surroundings that I did not notice you walking off. After a while I turned round and you were gone. I started following what seemed a main path through the quarry. I called your name.

As I took a left turn, the path narrowed a bit and became quite rocky and uneven. Nevertheless I followed it, as I was now intrigued by what was round the next corner. And there it was in front of me, almost life-size, on a large rock: a person falling.

I was so drawn to that sculpture that I sat down opposite it. This image of a person falling was exactly how I was feeling. Since my father's death I felt like I was mid-air. I did not feel grounded or settled any more. That's why I took my shoes off, to feel the ground beneath my feet and somehow feel rooted.

I sat there for a while, until I remembered that I was looking for you. I put my shoes on and started walking again. I got back to the main path and started shouting your name, when somehow – out of the blue – I tripped on a rock that stuck out of the ground and fell to the ground. I knocked myself out for a couple of minutes.

When I opened my eyes my knee hurt very much. My head was also quite sore. I had hit the ground, properly, with my whole body. I retrieved my phone from my pocket and called you. Within a few minutes you found me and took me straight to hospital.

Later that night, I limped out of hospital. I had stitches on my head and a bandage around my knee. I had finally hit the ground and woken up to reality. My father was dead and I had to get on with my life.

Three for the Pot
by
Sylvia Weston

The summer he was six, Dennis first began to learn the art of poaching. Putting several pairs of boots into a hessian sack, his father said, "Take these to the farmhouse, tell 'em the price is five and eight pence and come straight back with the money. Return across the fields, don't go wandering off through the woodland path."

Slinging the sack over his shoulder, the boy set off towards Martinstown. At the farmyard, the geese ran at him, gobbling and hissing. Dennis swung the sack to keep them at bay. Mrs Casey popped her head out of the back door and invited Dennis inside. He showed her the repaired boots and collected the money. As he left, she slipped some sweets into the empty sack.

Dennis set off back, dragging the sack behind him through the stubble. He was soon hailed by the local bobby and waited until the overweight and out of breath policeman caught up.

"What've yer got in that sack?" demanded the constable.

"Nothing to interest you," replied the boy cheekily.

"Don't you give me none of your lip. Empty it out 'ere on the ground." Dennis did as he was told, tipping out the sweets and shaking the sack to demonstrate that there was nothing else in it.

"I'm sure you've been up to summat, I think I'll escort you 'ome and have a word with yer father," decided the copper.

At home in the kitchen his father asked, "What 'ave you been up to, young Dennis?"

"Nuffin', Dad, I just delivered the boots as you said. Here's the money."

The policeman looked slowly around. "What 'ave you bin

up to, Fred?"

"Nuffin'. I bin 'ere all mornin', mending these 'ere boots." The policeman had another look round, grunted and then left. When the constable was out of earshot, Fred let out a hearty laugh.

He went over to one of two wooden sheds, unlocked it and lifted down a laden sack from a high hook. Three fine plump hens, still warm, rested inside. His wife asked, "'Ow did you get past the geese? D'int they raise the alarm an' the farmer's wife come out?"

Fred chuckled. "She came out alright, but all she saw was Dennis and took him inside. I was just out of sight, then I was in that chicken shed, wrung the hens' necks and was out again in a jiffy. I hid in the wood until I saw PC Barnes going 'ome for his dinner. He saw Dennis and was off after 'im. I had plenty of time to take the shortcut through the woods, put the birds in the shed an' get back to me shoe repairin'. That copper knew summat was up, but couldn't fathom what. Come an' 'elp me pluck they chickens and them'll be in the pot afore the farmer's wife even knows they're missing."

Walking along the Jurassic Coast
by
Georgia

Walking along the Jurassic coast is awe-inspiring; the city of sheer cliffs towers over me and the sea air drifts to the back of my throat. The sun slaps me in the face with its flaming hand and the forceful wind pushes me forward with a vigorous shove. I walk. I walk until my legs ache and my dog has stopped chasing his ball. The fishy smell is still blocking my nose and the ragged rocks are leaving blisters on my feet. I turn to face the tenacious winds and walk back. I am far from Lyme Regis and long past Charmouth; the sea is close to the cliffs and I am narrowly walking past without getting wet. I feel the soft brush of my dog which tells me he is close behind but I dare not look back because a single wave could easily take me out to sea.

There are soft rain drops on my head and before long, the heavens open up, and substantial rain falls at my feet, making the waves crash and the path perilous. Soon small rocks crumble from the top of the cliff and break into small sharp shards like glass. The sea is now nipping at my heels. My heartbeats are fast and short and I am out of breath. I know I am in real danger. I stumble a few times and graze my hands and knees. My legs are like jelly and, with the added stinging of my knees, I can hardly walk. I grab on to the cliff for extra stability but it just crumbles away. The sea has now risen to my ankles and I cannot see my feet or the ground. I am afraid there will be a giant hole which I will fall down and never be found. Every time I trip I have momentary flashbacks of my childhood and think I am going to die.

I fall; the water takes my breath away and the sea swallows me up. This time I know I am going to die. I think of my future; my husband and children, my family and friends and how I was going to travel and have a job. I am brought back to the present by my dog's barks which are getting farther and farther away. I have a mouthful of sea water which makes me gag. I swim upwards; I break through the water and take a gulp of air. I hear a loud splash, louder than the rainfall and the falling rocks, and then a tug on my arm; it pulls me to the rocks and I clamber up on to the cliff. I hear a deafening yelp and catch a sight of my petrified collie scrabbling above the waves until he's dragged under.

As Luck Would Have It
by
Kathy Hallsworth

Avril sat on a bench overlooking West Bay. Harvey, her five-year-old shoved chocolate ice cream in his mouth. His face radiated mischief, as always.

Yesterday this trip hadn't been planned, but after switching on the TV last night, and watching a programme called *Broadchurch*, Avril became impressed by the story's stunning location. The sweeping views of the coastline and harbour had stirred something inside her.

This morning her only desire was to go there. She lost no time getting Harvey and a picnic into the car. All the time singing, "We're off to the sea, sea, sea," and Harvey shouting back, "Take me, me, me." After ten minutes Harvey was asleep, helped by the steady motion of the car.

The roads were quiet, so it wasn't long before Avril thought about her mother, Gwen: how she loved early spring mornings, unknown destinations and adventures out of the house. They were so alike, strange really, considering she'd always known she was adopted. Making the 'nature-nurture' debate interesting. However, it wasn't until she became pregnant with Harvey that Avril gave any thought to tracing her birth mother. Then watching Harvey develop through his early years caused her to want to find out more. What had happened before Gwen and Dave had taken her for adoption, aged three?

The social worker warned Avril not to expect too much, but the brutal rejection letter from Maureen O'Donnell was gutting. Her birth-mother wrote, 'You came out of the worse period of my life, and in no circumstances do I want to return there'. Avril read the bitter phrases several times struggling to make sense of them. However, sitting there in the early morning sun, watching Harvey talk to another little boy struggling with a big crab net, made her smile. She felt contented for the first time since the letter had arrived.

The other boy's father sat on the opposite bench. They watched the two lads dump the crab net in favour of climbing the roped off slipway. Neither parent had seen the notice stating *Keep off the Fence*, so both were alarmed when an old gentleman lifted his walking stick, shouting angrily, "Little hooligans!"

Instantly, both parents were on the scene, protecting their sons from the old man who backed away cursing. Both boys started to cry, mirroring each other's mannerisms. Avril stared at their likeness as she said, "I'm so sorry my lad has led yours astray. He loves climbing, and I didn't think it could cause a problem."

The stranger replied, "Same here."

Together they comforted their offspring until Harvey's new friend boldly announced, "I'm Connor, Connor O'Donnell from Northern Ireland."

Avril, repeated the name slowly. "O'Donnell?"

His dad explained they were there on holiday and had decided to come and visit West Bay, on a whim, after seeing a television programme. It was Avril's turn to say, "Same here." Both parents laughed, recognising they seemed to have things in common, things worth discussing.

A Small Revolution
by
Jackie Burgoyne

Polly heaved open the door. A wedge of early morning light dropped across the wooden floor. The squeal of the hinges made her flinch. Don't be foolish, she told herself, no one's listening. The village hall was just as they'd left it, the pictures hung in the positions that the committee had decided, not those that she, the exhibition organiser, with her degree in art history and four years curating the Ashmolean collections, had suggested. She might have embroidered a scarlet letter on her chest. 'I' for incomer. 'I' for ignore.

In prime place and under the flattering light of a small window, was a contribution from the chairman of the Village Society, 'Bluebell Wood', purple scratches with trees, sky and clouds elaborated in a particularly cloying style. Around the walls, in steadily less prestigious positions, were efforts from the vicar's wife, the churchwarden, the head teacher and the major. Hung in the small, cold annex were just two: an evocation of a green man, each leaf painted tenderly by Sally, the dinner lady, and opposite that, a meticulous pencil drawing of St Anthony's Church, each detail brought alive; the perspective, light and shadow represented perfectly.

Polly thought of the efforts she'd made. Joining the Women's Institute and the Parent Teacher Association. Concocting a polite response to every tedious choice forced upon her by the book group. Hours spent hovering over marmalade, boiling it to a set for the horticultural show. At Christmas she'd written half a dozen messages in hand-painted cards, inviting this person or that for coffee and mince pies or a glass of sherry. None had replied.

She scraped the stepladder into position and poked the

large canvas from the wall. It fell with a satisfying crack. A few taps of a hammer and she had created hanging space for the two best pictures of the exhibition. She manhandled the bluebell monstrosity to the door. With a bit of a shove it should fold into the recycling bin. In one hour it would be transported on a tour of the surrounding villages, scraped by broken bottles in Bincombe, splashed with rotting food in Rampesham, finishing with a private exhibition at Dorchester's town dump. Polly imagined the look of confusion, then outrage, rolling across the chairman's face when he found her own and Sally's pictures in pride of place. She grinned. She hadn't grinned for ages. Enough of pandering to them, enough of trying to fit in. From now on that scarlet letter would be 'I' for incisive, 'I' for in charge.

The Gate
by
Ingrid Hayes

Wave upon wave lunged and pounded on to the Chesil shoreline, maliciously seeking out points of weakness in dips and hollows. Sal huddled in a ditch stream, waiting for the storm to turn, as waiting 'out' was what she did until she could scan the shingle for things that the storm felt free to offer her.

The pantomime of noise eased and Sal gathered up her sodden skirt and swiftly descended into the windless valley. Her numb fingers clumsily lifted the gate latch, whereupon an instant shaft of light revealed the dark shadow of her aunt.

"'Ad ye waitin' like a trembling lamb? 'Ee filled yer head wiz moonshine. No doubt 'e end upon them gallows afore too long, if 'e's not already swingin' in town."

Tears flowed freely, washing away her dream of leaving the shingled wasteland. A click, both women started: a latch dropped heavily. Aunt May held her breath...

***

The ebb and flow of the waves beyond the ridge could be heard from the house below, where now, in the deepening shadows, a tall, dark-coated figure looked out toward the dappled light and the shifting shapes of the trees.

***

In time – her eyes veiled – she breathed deeply of the salted air and then retreated slowly into the clinging darkness. She grasped the copper kettle and placed it heavily on to the hot plate, feeling the pulse of its watery content. Her despondent reverie was awakened by a sound, a distant unlatching of her heart, and she sensed his sea-chilled footsteps upon the path.

***

The sea-changes of time rippled through the wooded hollow until, at last, a lone traveller viewed the volley of light shafting along the ridge of hills before him.

The upland pasture reached the skyline then plunged abruptly into craggy fields. At the bottom of the sheer cut valley a dark patch of woodland encircled a stone ruin, whose only remnant of habitable existence was a striking chimney, proudly thrusting above the tree line. An instinct to follow this path overcame the importance of views. A path it was, or had been: clumps of handmade rockeries, laced with heather not common to this area, made him think that someone wanted to make this pathway welcoming. He surveyed the long forgotten vegetable patch and as the light dimmed he felt his presence somehow intruded upon the quiet. He turned quickly and in so doing caught his jacket on a nail, which had long ago supported a metal notice.

He felt an urgency to ascend swiftly out of this strange backwater, strode upwards to the harsh light of the beach and gratefully breathed in the salty droplets of the waves below.

He looked back down on to the grey ruin and thought he saw two figures by the gate. Quickly he turned and made his way to the shingled shoreline, leaving no trace of his watery footprints.

Love and Hate
by
Sheena Dearness

Summer holidays! They keep asking me what I want to do. There is only one thing an eight-year-old would want to do. Go to the beach and funfair of course. Grown-ups are weird.

Music is everywhere at Weymouth beach: loud, exciting, all mixed and mingled in hot air. My ten-month-old baby sister Chloe is with us.

Sparkling water inviting, my feet sinking into the sand as I run. I shriek. Brrr, it's cold. Teeth chattering, I emerge from the water; watch the droplets of icy cold water spill down my pale white board of a body. I check to see if they are watching 'me' or 'her'.

Today beach, tomorrow walking. I know they'll make me walk loads; it's their 'thing'. Rucksack on my back, obligatory chicken paste sandwiches and crisps, I trail along as they exclaim "Ooo" and "Ahh" at every opportunity. Even Chloe gurgles like a drain. Ugh.

Back on the beach I build an enormous sandcastle. I run to and fro to fetch water. Chloe shuffles her way onto the castle battlements. She's flattened my masterpiece.

"Look what she's done!" I scream.

"You can build another one, Jon," Dad mutters.

I roll in the sand with the despair of having a baby sister. Sometimes I just hate her.

Soggy sandwiches follow, mixed with gritty sand, smashed up crisps and the usual tussle with 'her' trying to grab my food.

"Watch your food! The seagulls swoop!" Mum cries. I wish a seagull would swoop my sister up.

We're going to Lulworth! Whoopee! Rock pools where I collect whelks and pick up baby crabs.

Chloe's crying. I cruelly wave a crab in front of her. She reaches to grab it. Everything goes in her mouth. Chloe with a crab inside her mouth. Hee hee. My mother glares. She's read my mind.

We're back on Weymouth beach. Hooray! I want to re-build my destroyed castle; this time, well away from that dratted sister of mine.

The beach is packed with people. I can't build anything.

At the funfair, the horses prance up and down, round and round. Endless races that finish nowhere. Nice to watch, but the flashing dodgems call.

"Move out of the way!" I scream as my car jostles and jolts. Dad's watching me. I wave.

Wispy curls of pink and white sugar magically form clouds of candy floss in a deep cauldron.

"I want some," I wail. What?! I have to share with Chloe? I giggle; it leaves sticky pink threads across her face.

The Dipper beckons.

"No, Jon. It's too dangerous," shouts Mum. "You're not old enough. Besides, Chloe needs feeding…" she tails off.

We trail to a café. She's in a high chair. I glare at her. She always spoils my fun. She can't even feed herself.

I hear them sniggering. Two kids opposite our table are pulling faces at Chloe.

Chloe's face crumples. She starts to cry. I move nearer her to block their view. Strangely I want to protect her.

How dare they! She's my sister!

The Nine Ladies
by
Martin Lake

Colin sat alone, his breakfast untouched before him. He gazed out of the window of the Little Chef in Winterbourne Abbas, watching the world pass him by: a soft sigh escaping his lips as another empty day loomed. Since his divorce he had little enthusiasm for life.

Suddenly, green eyes the colour of emeralds caught his. A girl stared self-assuredly at him from outside. He stopped, coffee mug forgotten, captivated. The girl turned, long black hair whirling in the sunlight. His eyes devoured her receding figure, committing every curve to memory as long slender legs stole her away.

She stopped unexpectedly, glancing back, melting him with a smile. Was that look for him? Was there a hint of beckoning in her deep green eyes? Only one way to find out, Colin thought, his lethargy dissipating. Leaving £10 on the table he hurried outside, fearful she might have gone. She was standing by the stile leading into the field, waiting. Her smile warmed him whilst her eyes dared him to follow. She turned, making her way towards the small wood across the field.

Who was she? Should he follow this beautiful, mysterious girl? Suddenly a purpose to his existence he hadn't felt for months breathed life into him. He didn't know or care why she wanted him, he simply exulted that she did. He followed, unable to resist her mystical allure.

At the wood's edge was a small area fenced off with metal railings. A rusty gate stood open. Inside were eight standing stones, placed in a rough circle with a large oak tree breaking the circumference. The tree was old and must have once been majestic but was now lifeless, branches devoid of leaves, boughs decayed and crumbling. The girl stood by the tree, her arms outstretched towards him. Her beckoning smile reinforced the invitation.

He stepped through the gate and went to her willingly, clasping her in an embrace. His eyes closed as their lips met. Rough bark of the tree against his back contrasted with her softness as she clung to him. Her smooth skin felt warm against his own. When did they undress? He didn't remember. The feel of her against him suffused him with joy. He dug his bare feet down into the soft loam, revelling in his oneness with the earth.

He knew her then, in that perfect moment. Knew who she was and what she wanted of him. He welcomed it. His spirit rose, soaring above her. He stretched, his arms reaching towards the sky, not arms but branches now, swaying in the breeze, new life already bursting forth. She stepped back, enraptured as she looked up at the newly reborn tree, before gliding over to the gap in the circle of stones. She re-joined her sisters, her body transforming as his had done, but differently. Shrinking in on herself, solidifying until she resembled the other standing stones.

And there Colin remained, silent protector standing watch over *The Nine Ladies*.

Storm in a Teacup
by
Eleanor Smith

They had walked to the end of the pier, and were leaning on the cool rails, watching the boats go by. The sun was washing the edges of the horizon, and the white cliffs in the distance were topped by a green swathe.

The bay reminded him of childhood holidays: the gritty sand beneath his feet, the refreshing gasp as he splashed in the waves, laughing with his sisters. He turned towards her.

"It's a good day for it. At least the sun is out." He could smell the tangy air.

"Yes," she said, wrinkling her nose. "At least that's one good thing."

The silence between them lengthened while the sun dappled the harbour and ripples gently formed, signalling the tidal surge into the sea. He watched as cormorants, black darts of birds, braved the cold water: disappearing and reappearing. He was fidgeting, his own unease spoiling the moment.

"I don't want to influence your decision, Marianne. You have to want it too." But as he said the words, his heart sank and his future disappeared into the suburbs of the Home Counties. "Maybe you will miss the big shops, the busy city life?"

She responded with a shrug that gave nothing away.

"And the job offer, well it's pretty good. Worth coming here… But I know it will be a very different kind of life." Her head was turned away, her long hair twisting in the breeze, as she walked in front of him, towards the café.

Suddenly everything looked dull to him, her lack of enthusiasm colouring his view. The sun went behind a cloud, and the colour seemed to leech out of the vibrant harbour scene. He sat despondently, stirring his tea. Her enigmatic smile was a mystery to him, and it was making him nervous. He stirred more sugar into his cup, creating a maelstrom, reminding him of the fickle nature of the sea and waves that sometimes crashed over the pier with such force.

"Well, have you decided?" His breath seemed to stop for a moment. Her amazing eyes opened wide and she slowly smiled at him.

"Darling, if you like it, I do."

No, this was not the right answer, he wanted confirmation that she too felt the magic of Weymouth, and that she really *wanted* this too. He stirred his tea again. This time the whirlpool in the tea was deep and wild. His expression was tense, his jaw clenched.

"I'm only teasing, Mark." She leaned back in the chair and laughed, and her long curly hair framed her face. "I LOVE it here! The sea, the beach, especially the harbour." She paused. "And it's a great place to bring up a baby." The spoon fell down on the saucer with a clatter, and he pulled her to him.

"Really?"

"Yes, really. In about seven months' time."

As he hugged her, Mark watched as the tea smoothed out, becoming a tranquil ocean.

Into the Sea
by
Martha

I take a step onto the promenade. I see the grey yet blue sky.
The birds on the beach are trying their hardest to set off in
the wind. I see the sun trying to decide its temperature for
today. I see the beach, the children running and screaming
with joy.

I take another step onto the beach. I feel the sand running
through my toes. The warmth and coldness of the still
undecided sun, and the wind rippling through my clothes
and playing with my hair.

I take another step onto the Cobb. I can smell that intense
salty incense of seaweed. I can see Lyme Regis so clearly
from here. I can see the arcades and the glorious two-sided
beach and the pastel coloured beach huts in rows.

I take another step on to the stony beach. I can hear dogs
barking, the people talking and shouting. I can hear the
seagulls robbing people of their lunch and the cars passing
by. I can hear the waves having battles amongst themselves
and the pebbles tumbling down on each other over and over
again to the circular motion of the sea.

The people, some cautious of the sea, keeping their
distance, and some best friends with it, willing to get lost in
the waves. Some in groups, some in pairs. Some only there
to stare.

I take another step next to the sea. I think how amazing it
would be to live there. Today it is so enchanting, so open
and full of things people haven't even heard of. The sea just
pulls you in, no one knows what's really out there. I want to
know. I want to swim with the fish and all the other
creatures. I want to ride a whale and feel the seaweed brush
against my legs every day. I do wish I could get away from
all the people and the struggles on land and move to a place

where there is danger, yet peace and beauty.

I take one last look at this place. I will never forget the busy arcades and the beautiful Cobb, or the unbelievable amount of memories. The rushing people racing by or the swaying, fish-ruled boats. Or the sound of the pebbles going in time with the sea, and the smell of the salty seaweed. I won't ever forget.

One final time I feel the warmth of the finally-decided sun. One last time I want to hear the stumbling of the pebbles. One last time I want to smell the seaweed. One last time I want to see the birds struggling to fly.

Now for the first time I want to see things that I've never seen before. I want to hear nothing but the sea. I want to feel the seaweed every day and I want to smell whatever the sea smells like.

I take one last step, one last breath. I step into that place I know I want to be. Into the sea.

Contributors

Abi enjoys all sorts of books and reads several within a short space of time. She is a keen writer and particularly enjoys writing non-fiction and free verse in poetry. Abi currently lives in the Netherlands but goes to a boarding school in Dorset.

Alfred is twelve and has been writing most of his life. He is an enthusiastic and keen writer. Sadly his dyslexia held him back in his younger life. But now he has conquered it. He likes to read action books, absolutely loves cricket and also likes swimming.

Becca is fourteen and lives in Wimborne. Her hobbies include ballroom/Latin dancing, singing and kayaking. When writing she loves exploring different aspects. There's a notebook by her bedside as she often has crazy ideas at 3am. She is currently working on her own book, so watch this space!

Ben is an enthusiastic writer and loves short stories. He has been learning English since he was five and really enjoys the subject. He also likes to play rugby in his spare time.

Ellis is fifteen, lives in South Dorset and enjoys blogging, drawing and going on adventures as well as writing short stories.

Georgia has loved writing for as long as she can remember. Her first story was in a scrapbook where it says: 'I went to the park' in very messy handwriting and scribbles that resemble flowers.

Laura has always loved books and writing. She enjoys bringing to life different characters in her stories. She was inspired to enter this competition as she wanted to share her love of Dorset and Corfe Castle. Still only fourteen, when not writing Laura enjoys drama and dance.

Louise enjoys reading particularly dystopian texts. She also enjoys writing stories in class. Louise loves acting, singing, dancing and photography.

Lucy enjoys reading and writing creatively, especially reading mysteries. Lucy writes because she can live another life through stories and through the characters she creates. She also enjoys dancing and acting because she can get lost in other worlds when she is on stage.

Martha enjoys reading, particularly horror and thriller books. She is a keen writer and enjoys writing using descriptive language and writing stories. Martha is thirteen and her other hobby is dancing and choreography.

Megan became interested in writing when a friend wanted help to complete a book. After this, Megan began writing her own stories in her spare time. Megan likes writing with and about her friends.

Natalya is a fifteen-year-old pupil from Sherborne Girls School in Dorset. She enjoys creative writing and her story is inspired by a trip around Pageant Gardens in Sherborne. She enjoyed writing the story as it made her look at things in more detail than when passing them every day.

Sam is twelve years old. His inspiration for writing comes from the author Rick Riordan. He has lived in many parts of Europe and in England, including Lulworth in a small thatched cottage. This is where he was able to draw most of his descriptions from.

Sophie, born in 1999 in the Midlands, moved to Dorset aged four. She attended schools in Wimborne, before moving to Parkstone Grammar School in 2011. She lives in Witchampton with her parents, two older sisters and a younger brother. She is an aspiring engineer with a love of reading.

Jude Alderman, a Dorset-based artist and writer, has been writing since she was twelve years old. She's a Thomas Hardy obsessive, sea-bird watcher, cliff-path walker, compulsive kitten-homer, chaser of rainbows and impossible dreams, and a hunter of fallen shooting stars.

Tod Argent (Tony McDonald) writes poetry, plays and short stories. After a career in the forces and then teaching, he started to write and joined the Writers' Study in West Moors, Dorset. For fun, he walks his dogs all over Dorset and is a sometime golfer.

Marianne Ashurst, a Lancashire lass at heart brought up in Blackpool (which accounts for her love of bright lights and all things glittery!), retired recently to enjoy seeing more of her granddaughters and devote time to writing.

Sharon Beauchamp was born and raised in Toronto, Canada. Travel and theatre occupied her early years, eventually settling in the UK and calling Dorset home with husband Tim and son Tom. Sharon recently retired from a long and happy career in nursing and now uses her third age to reflect, learn, explore and enjoy.

Thomas Beauchamp was born in Bristol before he moved to Dorset with his family. Recently completing a Physics degree from Oxford, Thomas, a Parish Councillor, is putting down roots in Dorset. A passion for politics, Thomas also loves cooking, the Dorset countryside and astronomy.

Mary Bevan promised herself to write as soon as she retired and has now got the writing bug! She has won several prizes for her short stories and flash fiction. She and her husband have lived in Dorset for almost forty years and love the county.

Louise Bliss lives in Dorset with her husband and two young children and finds Dorset's scenery and history a real source of inspiration. The idea for her story came from her interest in buildings set in the beautiful Georgian town of Blandford Forum.

Wendy Breckon lived in Hertfordshire with her husband Peter and her sons Sam and Oliver for many years. She enjoyed being Head of Drama, but was thrilled to rediscover the writing gene on arrival in the inspirational West Country.

Jackie Burgoyne writes on the Isle of Portland and is happiest when walking along the beaches and cliffs, thinking about character, setting and plot. Two short stories appear in an anthology published in aid of the Alzheimer's Society.

Rachael Calloway, primary school teacher, mum, avid reader and closet writer, can often be found in cafés – downing coffee and furiously scribbling. Her story is dedicated to her own mum who died of cancer and her dad who's bravely fighting it.

Mike Chapman, born in Kent, educated in Sevenoaks, Amiens and Cambridge University, graduated in rowing and English Literature. He's lived in Christchurch, Sturminster Newton and now Bourton, is married to Elaine and has a son from a previous marriage.

Gail Chappell, married with two grown-up sons and living in Bournemouth, works as a Learning Support Assistant with students with high functioning autism, Asperger Syndrome, language and communication difficulties. An avid reader she took up writing when her sons went to university and tries to write something every day.

Marion Cox, living in Dorset for over forty years, worked as a journalist for the *Dorset Echo*, the *Dorset Magazine* and as a freelance theatre critic. Like most writers, she's always on the lookout for stories and the plot for 'D-Day Landings' came from a local lady's wartime experiences.

Sheena Dearness has adopted Dorset as her home; she originates from the Orkney Islands which also have farmland and coastline but are flatter and much colder than Dorset! Being published by Dorset Writers Network is a delight.

Christine Diment, born in Johannesburg, South Africa, studied English and Drama at Sheffield University and at the Central School of Speech and Drama, London. A teacher of Drama and English she enjoys writing plays as part of She Writes and Juno Theatre, based in Salisbury.

Lisa Dixon, a freelance personal development and skills coach, moved to Dorset in 2013 after six years working and travelling the UK and Asia. Always interested in poetry and creative writing she joined a local writing group to share ideas with like-minded individuals.

Britta Eckhardt-Potter, originally from Germany, has lived in the South West of England for fifteen years and on Portland for the past seven. She loves nature and going for walks, which is why her favourite poets are Wordsworth and Coleridge.

Vivienne Edwards was born in Salisbury, and is married with five daughters. A retired social worker, with a love of genealogy, her vivid imagination has found expression through poetry and story-telling. Communicating the heart and voice of a character is one of Vivienne's great passions.

Claudette Evans, a gigging musician, decided to concentrate on teaching piano, guitar and vocals along with writing and recording her own songs. Whilst travelling with her terrier she discovered a desire to write imaginative, but informative stories through his eyes and experiences.

Elizabeth Friend is a self-development therapist and tutor. Since moving to Dorset in 2009 she has written several radio dramas and has presented her short stories to the public as a member of Story Traders. Last October she was long-listed for her memoir by *Mslexia* magazine.

Patricia Gallagher has lived in West Dorset for over 30 years and has recently moved to Crossways. She works for the County Library Service as well as for Dorset County Hospital Medical Library.

Madeline Goodey returned to Dorset seven years ago when she decided to stop teaching and spend more time pursuing her first love of painting. Her paintings often tell a story and recently she has started to explore the possibility of giving them a written voice.

Kathy Hallsworth has always found playing with words a creative pleasure, both as a lecturer in post sixteen education, and as a hobby. Part of a writing team in Bristol, she created cabaret material, pantomime sketches and one act plays. After moving to Bridport she started Story Traders.

Ingrid Hayes, originally from Manchester, has spent most of her working life in Dorset and Somerset. Now retired from teaching she is actively involved with adult literacy and other voluntary organisations. The link between people and landscape – her particular interest – features in her contributions for this book.

Heather Hayward, born in a farm cottage near Corfe Castle, Dorset, youngest of six children, went to school in Corfe and Wareham. Her knowledge of the Corfe Castle area is vast and her vivid memories of the 1950s prompted her to write 'The Village'.

Marlene Heinrich has made Dorset home for most of her life but she has also worked abroad in several countries. She started writing as a hobby when she retired and loves the impact it has on her.

Richard Hewitt began writing stories in his spare time about three years ago, shortly after relocating to North Dorset. After attending a Dorset Writers Network Short Story workshop he and Jane Wade began the eXchange Creative Writing Group. This is his first published work.

Martin Lake works as an IT Manager for a large law firm and lives in West Dorset with his wife and children. He only started writing seriously in 2014 after attending a local Creative Writing course and is delighted that his short story, 'The Nine Ladies', is to be published by the Dorset Writers Network.

Simon Leighton was born in Leicester in the early 80s then moved to his father's hometown of Weymouth with his family. Although life is very busy with work, social life and a four-year-old, he loves writing and fits this in wherever he can; preferably with a little music and a bottle of ale.

Jo Maycock, a retired primary school teacher, joined the local creative writing group in her village and found, to her great delight, the pleasure of writing. She now has her first computer and is excited by this whole new world that has suddenly opened up to her.

Sam Morley works in advertising and is therefore completely at home with works of fiction and suspension of disbelief. She has been to many weddings but sadly none like the one in her story.

Maya Pieris's book, *Take 6 Carrots, 4 Heads of Celery, 8 Large Onions*, blended food and history and took her mind off nappies, bottles and sleepless nights! Moving to Dorset in 2010 led to Dorset Voices, a self-publishing project and her first stage play and a cookery column for the *Eggardon & Colmers View* magazine.

Mona Porte, a teacher of languages, later specialised in teaching children with dyslexia. Her mother maintained that Mona 'had a book in her' so leaving teaching prompted her return to creative writing. In 2014, she received the Acorn Award for best unpublished writer in the Bath Short Story Competition.

Penny Rogers left the university library where she wrote books and journal articles for a professional and academic market, and began writing creatively five years ago. Since then her short stories, flash fiction and poetry have been published in print and online. Humour is never far away in her writing, even in the bleakest of situations.

Alison Scott has lived in many places but keeps coming back to Dorset. She loves the gentle landscape and the wealth of fauna and flora and is passionate about preserving it for future generations.

Eleanor Smith loves to write and is a member of the Chalkstream writing group. She lives by the harbour in Weymouth and is inspired by the harbour scene, as well as the beautiful Dorset countryside. She lives on a yacht for part of the year, which gives her space to think.

Cilla Sparks has lived near Wimborne in East Dorset for over thirty years. During that time there have been many changes to the town and surrounding landscape, but it is still beautiful. She worked as a teacher in Dorset schools, and as a therapeutic counsellor. Now 'retired' she runs two Writing for Wellbeing groups.

Elizabeth Thomas was born in Blackheath, London, but moved to Dorchester when she was five years old. For a few years she lived within a few hundred yards of Max Gate and early memories of glimpsing the house down the driveway influence her writing about Thomas Hardy. Returning to live in Dorset has jump-started her creative writing.

Anne Tillin is sixty-seven years of age, married with two daughters and four grandchildren. She retired this year from her occupation as a psychotherapist and has been part of the Colehill Creative Writing Group for eighteen months. A Future Learn course on writing fiction inspired her to start writing short stories.

Jane Wade, a published writer of short stories and novels, loves craftwork and design, knitting, mermaids, embellishing clothing with sequins and embroidery, and the colour red. After a lifetime's ambition she finally moved to Dorset (Sturminster Newton) in December 2013.

Carol Waterkeyn is, by day, an editor for a Dorset-based charity and was formerly a freelance journalist, PR/Marketing Officer and air stewardess. By night, she is an aspiring fiction writer with several prizes to her credit. Carol is a member of the Writers' Study writing group in West Moors, an avid reader, gardener and knitter when she's not writing.

Suzanne Webb has lived in many parts of the UK from Plymouth to the Hebrides and Norfolk to Glasgow before settling in Dorset where she brought up three wonderful children and is currently awaiting her first grandchild. Various hobbies and interests include walking in the countryside whilst attempting to capture the landscapes with her camera.

Sylvia Weston has been a member of a local writing group for about eight years and has recently joined a second one. She particularly likes to write stories based on real people and true events.

Denise Whittle, born 1949 in Boston, Lincolnshire, retired to Dorset six years ago, after life as teacher, carer, guitarist and writer of songs which she self-publishes on SoundCloud. She thinks the key to her writing is a desire to entertain, has no wish to tell the world great truths, and distrusts that motivation in artists.

Karen Wright lives in Bridport and draws on the local landscape for her inspiration. As well as enjoying the challenge of flash fiction, she is currently writing her third book for young teens in the *Abbotsbury Series* and is about to publish an illustrated story for younger children with Asperger's syndrome.

Robin Wrigley retired from a lifetime of working worldwide in the field of oil exploration. He joined the Wimborne Writers' Group in 2014.

This Little World

Strong sense of place is assumed and the unifying theme of disparate stories

I especially liked Alfred's "The Roman till" which adds another dimension - linking the location across two ~~two~~ eras, or ~~too~~ remembering those who have enjoyed or shaped the cristy in days gone by. A sense of history as well as place.

Not keen on cover - suggesting space - though containing DORSet views, they're lost amid complex design + too many images'

Touched by the unusual story of a German pilot responsible for bombing a DORset church in "October Journey' by Mary Bevan, and its conciliatory ending'
Stories of age - youth + connections passed down generations'
Life entwined (inseparably) with the setting as in "A Life' by Mona Porte - a certain magical realism.
Quote p 44.

Printed in Great Britain
by Amazon.co.uk, Ltd.,
Marston Gate.